A CHANGE OF

NEEDS

BY

NATE ALLEN

__Dedications__

To my father, for instilling in me the belief that I had a purpose;

To my brother, for believing in me when I had self-doubt;

To my son, for his inspiration and reminding me the only difference between believing and doing is trying;

To my nephew, for his audience, encouragement ...and letting me know when "doing" became <u>done</u>.

<u>Acknowledgements</u>

To my 10th grade English teacher Mrs. "A" for suggesting I might be incapable of writing anything of substance, and in the process letting me know that I could.

To my 12th grade English teacher Mrs. "G" for providing me a place to be creative when I needed to be someone other than myself, and letting me discover that you have to "crawl" before you can run.

CONTENTS

CHAPTER 1

SYNCHRONICITY

In the 1920's Psychoanalyst Carl Jung coined a phrase, "Synchronicity." To sum up the use and appreciation of the term here, the expression *"meaningful coincidence"* seems to capture the essence. In a world where we spend much of our time and energy searching for meaning in things where none exists, sometimes, quite serendipitously, we conversely find meaning, be it good or bad, in things that at first glance seem to be *"meaningless."* Whether you wish to call it "destiny," "fate," or mere "chance," the truth is that at the end of our days, perhaps some of the most significant occurrences, moments, and relationships in our lives are nothing more than just a matter of timing, a consequence of being in a certain place at a certain time ...*synchronicity*, as it were, or "meaningful coincidence" as the case may be.

To the people who knew him best, Jacob Garris Arnett was a smart, honest, dependable and caring man. An underemployed yet hardworking conscientious and trustworthy fellow with character, a loving devoted father, and friend... The kind of man you could leave your wife and kids with ...and to be sure he **was** all of those things. But there was another side to him as well, the *"yin"* to that *"yang"* which was not clearly visible, nor entirely yet developed or revealed to himself even, which was capable of jealousy, deception, vengeance, and ...obsession. Things which were entirely unthinkable and contrary to his conscious self and the man he thought himself to be, contrary to the image of the man whom he wanted to be seen as, and yet, as we all are, he was just a work in progress and malleable ...and as time would reveal, the people who thought they knew him best, didn't *know* him as well as they *thought*.

He was on an upward swing in his life when he met her, having recently returned from an adventure abroad, the intended goal of which had not been accomplished, but the attempt itself had proven to be quite beneficial for him. In many ways, over the

2

course of a life, failure often proves to be a much better teacher than success, and out of it many things can be learned, suffice it to say he'd had the opportunity to learn much in his life, better to have tried and failed, he thought, than never to have tried at all.

Generally speaking, it was a time when most of the things in his life were going quite well, family, work, women. For a man of forty-five he was literally in the best shape of his life, and it showed. When he walked into a room, people took notice, the women ...for the reasons women take notice, but the men as well, after all, it is the nature of the beast to size up the competition and measure oneself against it, and he represented a level of competition. Upon close examination he was not a pretty man, his flaws were many, and yet he wore them well. If scars are the sign of a man of character, willing to fight for what he believes, then he resembled such a man. A faint crescent shaped indentation under his left eye, from the ring of a man who had long since died of unnatural causes bore testament to the fact. To be certain, it was not the individual aspects of him that could be dissected and appreciated or admired, but the "whole" of him as it were, from a physical standpoint, was more impressive than the sum of the individual parts. At 6ft, 192 lbs, he had the profile of a man who looked like he could be a handful if called upon, and he knew it. At a time when many of his peers were having mid-life crises, he was quietly, unbeknownst to anyone, having a mid-life "free-for-all," on a roll, ladies and lust in relative abundance as it were ...having the time of his life.

She, on the other hand, was on an admitted and self-proclaimed downward swing in her life. Stuck in a seemingly stale marriage that had unnoticeably and unremarkably morphed from love into what can best be described as a necessary friendship, with three children years from leaving the nest. The growing disappointments of a life full of promise which seemed now stifled and unfulfilled, she felt as a prisoner to her perceived happiness, and the charade of it all, the weight and burden of which had left her with understandable bouts of depression, at times just short of what seemed like an inevitable nervous breakdown, but, to her credit, short of it nonetheless. On the surface hers' was a story which was unfortunately not atypical of many a woman in mid-life, or a Dr. Phil episode for that matter, but as time would tell, there was absolutely nothing typical about Rae Anne Johnston beyond the appearance of things. If she'd been asked she would probably have described it very simply and succinctly as her "needs were not being met, and that was causing her some issues." Issues she was seeking to resolve, and which would give rise to this story. To lend some perspective and orientation to this picture, a legend to the map so to speak of this journey, at its onset they were going in opposite directions, one heading up, one going down ...and for a time, a time that would prove to be one of the most emotionally gratifying and yet painful of his life, they were stuck on the proverbial elevator of life together. This is a recounting of what followed.

It was a Saturday night in late October, a couple of days before Halloween, a beautiful time in North Carolina. Jake was making what had become a twice monthly pilgrimage from Franklin County to Raleigh because ...quite simply, there was nothing to do, no nightlife to speak of in Franklin County aside from a couple of local haunts, which were over-fished and the patrons too familiar. Franklin County was in no short measure a great place to raise a child, an increasingly popular rural bedroom community adjacent to Raleigh and Wake County that was growing out of the sheer fact that Raleigh had become too expensive for most working class families to live in it. Beyond that, it was not a particularly great place to be a divorced middle-aged man, it literally seemed as if the only single women there were either living with their parents ...or collecting Social Security.

Over the course of the past year, he had begun to venture out with more frequency. His role as parent had hit a level point, his ex-wife was at a good place in her life, and the custody situation of their son had balance and routine to it, affording him the opportunity to get out a bit more socially. Being the capital of North Carolina, Raleigh to many represented the face of the burgeoning "New South" and as such it offered a fair amount of variety for nightlife. As the population of the area had continued to boom, so had the choices, though to be fair and accurate, it was still at heart a college town and yuppie destination, and the slice of that pie which was geared towards adults in their 30's, 40's and beyond left something to be desired. Over the course of that time he had sampled nearly everything it had to offer with varying degrees of success, but had eventually become something of a regular, shameful as that sounds, at a couple of places. One in particular called Leon's.

It was a surprisingly eclectic establishment, offering great food, good music via a local band or DJ on the weekends and what he likened to a Playboy mansion-esque atmosphere, *sans* pajamas, of casualness and intent. The structure itself resembled something between a scaled down replica of a southern plantation house, and the stereotypical upper middle-class North Raleigh home on steroids, nestled unnoticeably on a wooded corner lot beside a day-care and a quarter mile from elementary and middle schools. It was unique in the nightscape of the area because of the coziness, wide range of ages, incomes and backgrounds, all very comfortably mingling and mixing together. People came there knowing this, and perhaps more importantly because of it. Always a diverse crowd ranging from people in their 20's to people in their

60's. Executives, executive-wannabe office types, blue-collar folks like himself, college students and a biker contingent all frequented the place, each respectful of the other, and crossbreeding like primitive tribes.

It was also logistically speaking the closest nightclub one encountered coming from where he lived, and proximity had its value and importance, driving late at night was always a concern and consideration, especially when traveling through an *über* policed town like Wake Forest. This particular evening like any other, Jake strolled in through the lobby and dining room into the tavern area, glancing around the room to see what the night had to offer in terms of ladies, and yes, making note of the ratio. It was by all accounts a good night to be there, the place was lively and loud, and the numbers were in his favor. He had not even made his way to the bar when he first noticed her, sitting tucked away in the corner with several of her girlfriends.

She had not dressed to go clubbing, or gotten "dolled-up" as it were, but modestly, like on a girls' night out, as it in fact turned out to be. She was a spectator to the human game of chess at hand, and his entrance had not gone unnoticed by her. While she sat there giving the appearance of listening to her girlfriends' idle chat, her eyes and a wry smile fell on him, not in an overtly flirtatious "come hither" or inviting way, but more likely as though she were unconscious and unaware of it. He sized her up as men routinely do, she was attractive, very attractive, but it took a discriminating eye to recognize it. Not because it was a subjective beauty, but on this outing disguised, subtle and downplayed, not unlike the understated schoolmarm in a Van Halen "Hot For Teacher" video. He thought she looked ready to bloom.

She was wearing comfortable clothes, which he would later learn, didn't do her voluptuous figure any justice whatsoever. He was wearing a long sleeve thermal shirt that served its purpose on the autumn eve, yet intentionally revealed a hint of the chassis he had built beneath it, faded jeans and a pair of sixteen year-old sharkskin boots that fit his mood on this occasion.

If "*All the world's a stage and we are merely players...*" then nightclubs are its "improv," countless dramas, comedies and one-act tragedies simultaneously playing out all at once, complete with the ever popular impersonations, people either pretending to be someone they're not, or who they think someone wants them to be on any given evening, all in the name of lust and hopes of getting laid, and everywhere critics. Leon's had no shortage of "characters."

It had been a long hard week, as a self-employed landscaper, the fall is a busy time, aerating, seeding, and fertilizing are hard but necessary work before the onslaught of leaves makes the work impossible and takes a precedence all its own, and this year in late October, there was an increased sense of urgency to get the one done before the other occurred. It had been a dry year, unusually dry, and the leaves had turned colors early and in doing so, shown their intentions of falling early as well. It was a time when he was still cutting grass, and yet doubled with the task of sowing the same thirty lawns so that his customers would have need of his services come spring. It was laborious, and he

10

sometimes enlisted the help of day laborers that could be found at an unofficial, yet well known labor drop-off point near Cabarrus Street on the fringe of southwest downtown Raleigh, just blocks from the Municipal Building, the Amtrak station stood as a backdrop to what often sadly looked like a modern day Hoover-ville.

Raleigh had experienced enormous growth the previous decade, and continued to. It was the type of growth that other areas of the country had to be envious of, but it had not been a universal prosperity. To those native to the area like himself it had seemed destined to, the proximity to three major universities and diverse research institutions, the World-renowned Research Triangle Park that they collectively fed and had given rise to, an educated workforce, combined with a temperate climate, and location, location, location. Mountains to the west, the Atlantic to the east it was naturally beautiful.

North Carolina, as one of the original colonies was steeped in history and tradition, and yet it was in many ways not unlike the image of Mayberry that

The Andy Griffith Show had painted it to be, Raleigh seemed like the world's biggest small town, with growing pangs and aspirations and apparently there were signs all over the country pointing toward it, **RALEIGH, NC 2342 MI**, etc.

The northeast must have been littered with them, NY, NJ, PA, Ohio, and the list goes on and on, or so the license plates on the beltline would indicate. No state was safe from Raleigh and the Triangle area extending a welcoming hand. Rest assured, it's true that you can't keep a good thing secret, and Raleigh and North Carolina had historically been the country cousin that other more metropolitan areas had not taken seriously, a place visited on vacation, but not invited to the table at the big house so to speak.

It had not happened overnight, but had been long in the making, life in the South has historically been slow, and while it was quickly picking up pace, it was largely of our own design and architecture. The tenets of what had made the area unique remained in place, and as a southerner, patience, while unnatural to humans in general, was part of the culture. Things didn't always get done when you wanted them to, but they got done. The area had waited its turn, and was now getting a lot of national recognition, and happily welcomed the unemployed looking for opportunity, the wealthy looking for continued prosperity... (And to show us how its properly done,) the middle-class Northern Urbanites looking for greener grass, or at least *some* patch of it, and the retirees looking for a comfortable alternative to Florida, Arizona, etc., to spend their golden years. All willing and able to pay their taxes, spend their disposable income, feed the local economy, etc. And to be sure, once the migration had begun, there was no shutting the door.

The continued acclaim became a priority and monster fueling itself. The City Administration seemed to have an obvious and undeniable "pissing contest" with its regional neighbors, Richmond, Charlotte, even Hot'lanta. And its propaganda-publicity campaign had worked, almost too well, to the point the growth was on the verge of exceeding the infrastructure necessary to sustain it. In reality the majority of the companies that came, brought employees with them, and the really "good" jobs they created, were of a high-tech nature that folks like Jake were not qualified for, nor could directly benefit from, only indirectly as unskilled entry level jobs in their plants and facilities or by result of the construction itself, building their homes, or like he, mowing their yards and landscaping their upscale lawns. It was a time when artisans and tradesmen prospered, plumbers, carpenters, painters and the like, made a slew of money and fallow tobacco fields took on romantic names as new neighborhoods and million dollar subdivisions, the previously land-rich/cash poor became new players in the local economy.

After a particularly strenuous week, he was too exhausted to put on any "airs" when heading out. It was an occasion that provided a fair and accurate representation of him, genuine and unpretentious, and I am certain that was of some importance as to what would later transpire. Like her, there was nothing typical about the man, beyond the physical outline of him and the simple initial assessment, he was a complex contradiction, like that curious item at a yard sale that you keep revisiting and examining, trying to make sense of and determine its value and worth. There was more to him than meets the eye ...mostly in a good way, though unknowable future events might require some amendments to his personal constitution.

He had played many roles in his time before deliberately heading down this difficult, wonderful, yet narrow path he now called his life, and in the process pissed away more opportunities than most individuals get in a lifetime, but tonight he was simply a man looking to get lucky, and she wasn't getting up from her perch, and he wasn't about to intrude, so upon finishing his beverage he proceeded to the dance area, to the chessboard so to speak, to participate in the game at hand.

As the night progressed and closing approached he found himself in the company of two women in their 30's, one attractive, one not so attractive. The attractive one he had met months before, her name was Lisa, or Leslie? ...and that in its entirety was all he knew about her, except as he recalled, she sometimes hiccupped when she giggled. He had nearly sealed the deal with her when her less attractive friends saved her from his lecherous intentions. He had later wondered if she hiccupped at other inopportune times, and tonight thought he might solve that mystery. She had brought along her equally amorous friend Grace, that name he was certain of, as he couldn't help but notice her lack of it, and the three of them were moving around on a sparsely occupied dance floor, like they were all ready to get naked and jump in a pile.

Lisa/Leslie was an honest "7" and Grace a "5" and in that convoluted and politically incorrect math that occurs everywhere at closing time, they were a collective "6" which seemed like it had all the promise of an unholy night ...but then he saw her again. She was now standing at the edge of the dance floor leaning against an empty booth, smiling to herself, enjoying the spectacle of it all, like a child in "time-out" sitting on the bench at the playground wishing she could join the fun, but prohibited from doing so. She was alone at the moment, no friends to run interference or complicate the conversation, fend off unwarranted advances like girlfriends sometimes do, and as one song ended and another began, he seized the opportunity to approach her, leaving the girls dancing by themselves until they eventually noticed his absence, and upon doing so took off to land elsewhere like barflies. *"I'm Jake"* he said, extending his hand to shake hers, and noticing the wedding band in doing so. *"I'm Rae Anne"* she replied, he paused for a moment, struck by the irony of it. *"That's interesting, my father's name was Ray, and my mother's name is Ann, nice to meet you Rae Anne."* *"That's more than interesting."* she chimed back, I was named after my father and mother. They shared a comfortable laugh for two people who had just met, each simultaneously recognizing the extraordinary chance of it all, she thought of it as a *coincidence* ...he would think of it as *meaningful*. In the matter of about a minute and a half she had managed to make him nervous, perhaps not overtly so, but nonetheless he felt the tension radiating from his neck down his spine to his limbs. It was a compliment to her and his immediate attraction towards her, it was rare in his adult life, and it excited him. Though it's in our nature to extinguish the feeling, fight or flight syndrome so to speak, he welcomed it, it was a good kind of nervous, and he struggled to conceal it for fear of how she might perceive it.

While he on the one hand looked better from a distance, she was now uncomfortably more striking the closer he got, full, pursed lips, green eyes, and dark hair and her body was womanly. Everybody has their type, or types as the case may be, and it was as if he had designed her for himself. If he had been a caveman he would have clubbed her over the head, tossed her over his shoulder, and carried her back to the cave where they would've lived happily ever-after and proceeded to populate the planet, that not being a viable option however, small talk leading somewhere seemed like the next best choice in his entranced state.

A short friendly conversation about the usual stuff, which he would remember nothing of, followed an unnaturally natural path, like dance steps painted on an Arthur Murray studio floor, all the while recognizing he was probably moments away from turning into stammering King George and looking creepy in the process. But he was maintaining, holding his composure, until she touched his hand, not once but twice, and while in a semi-paralytic state he still had the thought processes available to him to recall a **Men's Health** article about body-language which suggested that if a woman touches you three times... *&?+#*% ...his brain scrambled, during an initial meeting, it means she wants to have sex with you.

In that moment, he retreated to instinct, and in what had become his usual *modus operandi*, he told her he had enjoyed meeting her, and wondered if she'd like to continue the conversation another time. Instead of being forward and asking for her phone number, he proceeded to write his email address on a cocktail napkin and give it to her, jgarnett@email.com, and she in turn, without hesitation gave him hers, touched him on the hand ...and then politely excused herself as the posse of girlfriends had now approached, taking a defensive posture, and looking rather annoyed.

He stood, as the place began closing around him, not unconfused, trying to make sense of what might have just happened, and the dilemma it could present. His thoughts were riled up, and his mind congested like a coliseum lobby full of rowdy teenagers waiting for the doors to open to a rave or concert, unable to distinguish one idea from the next. All the while, The **Cowboy Junkies** *"A Common Disaster"* was playing in the background like a siren foretelling of things to come.

CHAPTER 2

FIRE ALARM

There are a number of things synonymous with the South and North Carolina, things other regions of the country associate with it, beyond its ugly past. Among a few of the more common are tobacco, the unmistakable accent, NASCAR, College Basketball, and Southern Baptists. It is after all part and parcel of the Bible belt, and she had been born the daughter of a well-known and much respected local Baptist Preacher, Raymond Waters. Rae Anne Waters, the "preacher's daughter," ...it has a mythical, almost *urban legend* distinction all its own.

As might be expected she had grown up sheltered, in an older established neighborhood in Raleigh, the house itself was the church parsonage, but she would call it home until she left for college just across town. It was an upbringing that would give her a strong foundation, and while she would *lose her religion*, or at least call it into question as she grew into adulthood, she would never lose her sense of family, of responsibility, and the strength it gave her. As a young child the neighborhood children couldn't pronounce Rae Anne but the resulting effort produced a nickname that would follow her, Raen, (pronounced rain) which as an adult, like most such nicknames, was reserved for her closest and oldest friends ...like the girls at the bar.

As an only child she was immensely loved, cherished, and adored. She had been a good student, loving respectful child, a "good girl," yet not at all entirely by her nature it seemed, but by effort. She had not disappointed her parents growing up, though being the daughter of such a man had its expectations and inhibitions that were contrary to her inclinations. As she matured, it would give her father reason for concern. The boys, like mosquitoes at dusk after a late afternoon summer thunderstorm, came around, all seeking some relief from their adolescent heat wave in the form of Raen Waters. None of which were ever satisfied, but the taunts and teases were abundant... though they were all sure to be careful of the old man. We have all known girls who developed early and yet did not evolve into the women we envisioned or expected, hoped or dreamed, peaking early as they say, but like an Encore Azalea, Rae Anne would bloom twice, …in the spring, and again in the early autumn of her life.

If there is some sort of hierarchy to describe a woman's desirability, then sexy supercedes beauty, and sultry trumps them both, not necessarily a balance of the two or even a truly high degree of either is required, it is a sexual confidence manifesting itself in an attitude. An intangible, it is difficult to define since the ingredients and recipe are unique to each woman in possession of the quality. Hers suggested a hint of controlled recklessness, voluntary prohibition, words that make no sense together, but considering her childhood, like the schoolmarm analogy, the preacher's daughter, …they did in regard to describing her, or as he would come to know her, and he would know her more honestly, and what she would be capable of than anyone else in her life, more than she would ever admit.

She was the kind of woman likely to say what was on her mind, not reflexively but thoughtfully so, yet it was often what she didn't say that was truly important. Like a seasoned politician she could be honest yet not entirely truthful, with an uncanny ability to edit herself even in emotional exchanges so as not to cause some impediment to achieving whatever her goal and purpose happened to be. She spoke with a careful *southern twang*, careful, because she never seemed uncertain of what was coming out of her mouth, and he would never hear her apologize for anything she had said, only the way it had been interpreted.

Sultry, in all its glory, did not only allow for imperfections, it didn't seem to exist without them. Sometimes it was an overbite, a raspy voice, a scar with some tragic story attached, one of hers was a tooth, just slightly crooked, to your left as you faced her, that ruined the symmetry of her smile but gave it character and not as a distraction. She had grown to smile a little crooked as a child in a self-conscious attempt to hide it, but as an adult it presented itself as a hint of delightful wickedness, and it gave the impression that she knew a secret and wasn't telling.

Ambitious, for a time she had worked in the weather department at a local TV station, an intelligent young woman, she had always been interested in science and meteorology, and had graduated from college with an undergraduate degree in Atmospheric Sciences, she hoped one day to work for the National Weather Service, EPA or FEMA perhaps, and all were realistic goals, and as luck would have it, she was given the opportunity to fill in on the 11 o'clock spot one evening when the weatherman failed to show. She nailed it, and eventually had the weekend morning slot. With an exploited childhood nickname like Raen Waters …how could she miss? Not a cloud in her sky …the future looked *bright*.

Frank Mangum was a fixture in the local community, "hell," he was a fixture in the region. For the past 14 years he had been the station's 6:00 and 11:00 sports desk anchor. He had played college basketball somewhere in the Big 10, Pac 10 or something like that, gotten into broadcasting, and wound up on Tobacco Road right in the thick of college hoops. He was well liked and more importantly respected by the area coaches, and thus entrenched in the local sports scene, yet in an unbiased way that someone from the area might be expected. It gave him credibility, and his audience and peers accordingly afforded him due respect. He was a good-looking guy, and it seemed like he never aged. Those of us who watch the news almost forget these people have families and real lives, and behind the scenes he and Rae Anne would become romantically involved, the knowledge of which only became apparent to their co-workers when an unexpected pregnancy arose.

He was married, and a quiet and very localized scandal ensued all while the rest of us were checking in to catch the scores, highlights, and tomorrow's forecast, oblivious to it all. Fair or not, by virtue of his visibility and tenure he was of greater value to the affiliate, and presumably had some leverage of an assumable nature that required those who make such decisions to overlook his indiscretion, though truth be told, they were probably envious and high-fiving each other at the revelation when having drinks after work. But she on the other hand would be unable to hide her "*involvement*," and right or wrong, while not fired, she was soon "off-the-air" so to speak.

In his defense, Frank had fallen in love with her and divorced his wife without as much drama as one might think, a childless union, the dissolution was fairly businesslike... Rae would later confess she thought there must've been something going on at the wife's end as well, a handsome landscaper trimming the bush perhaps, and they married as soon as the divorce was final, but after the baby came, a son, Franklin, called Frankie, followed by another child soon after, whom they named Raymond James, after both their fathers... (Not the NFL stadium as people first thought), and they called him RJ for short. They lived a happy life, though he was sixteen years her senior he didn't look it, and they made quite the couple. But marriages, as anyone who's ever been married can attest to, are difficult to maintain, and Frank, being a local celebrity had his share of news groupies, which came with its distractions, temptations, opportunities ...and eventual problems and excuses.

27

Past behavior being the best indication of future behavior, a suspicious Rae would find him one afternoon all bowed up at the Velvet Crown Inn with a local hockey team cheerleader, whereby she precipitously melted _down_, or blew _up_ depending on your perspective. Their marriage of three and a half years came to a close. The relationship that had been born in infidelity, ended with infidelity as well, and as ironic as it would prove, she had a strong aversion to unfaithfulness and being cheated on. The incident scarred her it seemed, and even to this day she still had not gotten over it on some level. It had not been a blow to her confidence, that remained intact as she attributed the waywardness to his apparent stupidity, but it had damaged her ability to trust her instincts and intuition for a time. She had the appearance of strength in the aftermath, but it was really a fear of being vulnerable and a fierce determination not to be again. Reconciliation not being an option for her, they would eventually come to an agreeable parting for the benefit of the boys as divorced parents are often forced to do, and while it was not easy, they worked hard to maintain a good relationship in that regard, and the children grew up happy as a result.

Local TV personalities make more money than we sometimes think, especially in a top 30 market like Raleigh-Durham, and Frank acted responsibly in that regard, and child support and alimony were provided. Finances consequently were not the real issue for her in the wake of divorce, instead for the immediate future she would need the stability of a man emotionally supportive, and trustworthy ...she found that in Glen Johnston.

Divorce, and the drama it had brought left her looking for answers, not uncommon, and in a characteristic effort to satisfy and understand some of the questions it had left her with, she went back to school part-time, not in pursuit of a degree, but as a matter of introspection and self-awareness. She didn't trust it to someone else like a therapist to tell her the "why" or "what" of it all, she needed to discern those details for herself, and correct them.

More than a mere comely young divorcee, she was the quintessential M.I.L.F., and commanded all kinds of attention. Never acting out of desperation or loneliness, she was commendably true to herself and her responsibilities to the boys, she chose her partners, few though they were, cautiously. Like everyone she had her "types" that she gravitated towards, a predisposition it would seem for authority figures, older men, and bad-boy alpha males, the only common denominator being that they had to be able to carry on an intelligent conversation. She would eventually come to find something of what she sought, short-term perhaps, in Glen, her Developmental Psych professor. They would have a brief courtship before a Dillon South Carolina marriage and Myrtle Beach weekend honeymoon, and not long afterwards a daughter together, Natalie. However, for a psychology professor he wasn't particularly insightful or intuitive. Perhaps because he dealt so much in theories and large schemes, that he missed the nuances of his own relationship, the warning signs, or billboards as they came to be, or perhaps, he would come to know after the fact he was simply out of his league with the woman. Intimidated by her on a number of important levels, and that seed of self-doubt, once planted in a man, cannot be unsown, and if unable to *weed* it out can render him incapable of satisfying those all important needs. And before long this marriage went the way of many others, becoming routine, emotionally vacant and impotent, and leaving some things to be desired by our gal Rae Anne, much as she may have in fact designed it. Enter our man Jake stage right...

He was different, and he knew it, how could anyone have come out of the confusion that was his childhood and not have been. He understood others' efforts and inability to categorize him, but he cared very little about it and made no apology for it. "He was who he was," and he didn't ask for, nor need understanding, only acceptance. While the sixties and early seventies are often remembered as a simpler time, before the dime-store became the dollar-store, when TV was black and white, carpet was shag, Playboy was risqué, and pornographic miniature playing cards were the most coveted currency of elementary school playgrounds, they quickly became a confusing time, a period of transition, struggling to make some sense of the explosion of culture, drugs, sex and the war in

Vietnam. The era exposed the same complexities of life that had always existed, only less publicly, and brought them and the imperfections of the illusion of family life out into the open, try to think of it if you can as a black and white Kodak moment meets YouTube.

Named after his father's brother Jacob, and Garris after an Army buddy who had died in WWII, he had grown up in a middle class home in Guilford County, North Carolina, the son of two loving parents who did the best they could in terms of raising him. But he had come late in their lives, at a time when they thought having a child impossible, and both in their forties ...at a time when they didn't have the energy for one and as is sometimes the case, for better or worse, the older boys in the neighborhood would have a greater influence on his upbringing. He was an innately happy child, confidence was in his genetic make-up, his personal composition, but life seemed to be continually tripping him up and throwing obstacles in front of him and much as the acorn has the promise of the strength of an oak, it would be years in developing.

His parents had their shortcomings like everyone. His father was a brilliant, gentle man, one of the strongest men he would ever know, mentally and physically, but he had one great weakness and that was his wife Ann, and she would exaggerate other weaknesses in him. Ann wore the pants in the family. Jake could never decide whether it was simply apathy that she hid behind a professed wall of fear and overprotection or just perhaps that at her age she was not willing to be bothered and burdened with the commitments that come with allowing a child to participate in certain activities, but for whatever reason, he wasn't allowed to do much, to pursue natural inclinations. *Needs* and *wants* can be squelched, but are difficult to eradicate and just as the roots of a stout tree will push up the sidewalk, like the weed that appears in the cracks, he would begin to assert himself as a teenager.

When the people who are supposed to provide you the things necessary and particular to your individual development don't, as a matter of survival and necessity one learns to persuade others, individuals who are not obligated to do so by ties of blood or family to do them for you instead, and he became very adept at the skill and grew from a very endearing boy to a genuinely endearing man. It was a quality that would prove to be a great asset. While it's important to instill confidence in a child, like anything that is given, it can also be taken away, but the confidence that comes from within, from surviving, with overcoming obstacles, born not only of success but of trying and failure, is much more enduring, and that is the confidence which would come to him, even if only realized much later in his life as a man.

After High School he attended a small Liberal Arts college, it was a school that had a reputation as an elite academic institution, and the curriculum, combined with his lack of discipline and abundance of appetite for all things, made his stay short. He bounced around from job to job, trying a bit of everything, in small doses. He would prove to have a short attention span when it came to many things, and employment was among them. Like many young folks, he knew not what he wanted to do, but he was quick to learn what he didn't.

He would meet his wife, Rene, when he was home one weekend for his 10th High School class reunion. He was twenty-eight and she twenty-four, a hostess at the Country Club the event was held, and nursing student at an area community college near Greensboro. In typical whirlwind fashion they fell in love and successfully carried on a long-distance engagement for a year until her graduation before getting married and moving to Raleigh. The boy came two years later and solidified the union for a time, but as he was finding to be formulaic in his relationships, it would have an expiration date, and those married couples that don't grow in the same direction grow apart. Five years into it they would part before irreparable animosity took root. He would readily concede she had been a good wife and a loving mother, and he would prove to be at best a dedicated father and *great* ex-husband. The period following the split and leading up to our story characterized by efforts to improve on his shortfalls, and the romantic landscape littered with one-night stands, brief, invisible and *meaningless* relationships. At which point our vixen enters stage left …and everything was subject to change.

He would spend the next day trying to focus on the tasks at hand, caring for his son, on auto-pilot regarding work, it was after all generally mindless physical tasks. He was conflicted about the situation, the only time he had ever been involved with a married women was unknowingly. She had told him she was legally separated …but apparently neglected to tell her husband, and that oversight had resulted in a very awkward conversation with an irate man on his doorstep while she lay naked and concerned in his bed.

On this instance however, still in the conceptual phase, it presented a different problem on his proverbial porch so to speak because it was inherently at odds with the image of the straight-up kind of guy he thought himself to be. But sometimes in life, situations arise where we are forced to make decisions …*difficult* decisions that require us to make a conscious choice to either abandon some aspect of our principles or personal code, or abandon those things which we desire with such fervor that it's simply reduced to a question of betraying oneself, or committing to violate another in the pursuit. To step across the boundaries we have drawn around our lives that define us as individuals and willfully trespass. And while he didn't even "know" the damn woman yet, the image he had concocted of her in his mind and the idea of who she might be, who she might become in his life, had infected him and he was now debating those selfish considerations all because of the touch of a hand …and the *nervousness* it had produced.

Almost immediately, he found himself incapable of coherent thoughts beyond the necessary and immediate, until he would take the next step out of an unavoidable curiosity to see what, if anything lay down the proverbial rabbit hole. He had gotten into the habit of offering women his email address in part because he was flirtatiously coy, but the gesture had largely become his signature move because he could twist a phrase *quite* well, and some situations had time constraints or extenuating circumstances like this one that required further negotiations. He had found the approach to be disarming to many women, less forward, unique and more *importantly* …it put the decision to advance things squarely on them, and their subsequent participation signaled a necessary level of interest and potential for *fun*.

It was a medium that allowed him to highlight the more attractive aspects of himself …a clever wit, boyish charm, and an intelligence that wasn't visibly apparent in his rough-hewn exterior. It afforded him the opportunity to write it, wait, revisit it and rewrite it as necessary, carefully crafting each note with some specificity toward the woman of interest, a comment about her eyes, her hair, an inviting smile or laugh …some uniquely captivating feature, relating it to the occasion they had met, etc., touching some part of them with his words. It was foreplay of a different sort, like preliminary pillow talk before the act itself …or a *figurative* hand already inciting lust underneath the skirt.

He would often cut and paste large pieces from emails he had sent other women. On some level it must've resembled a chain letter of sorts, a romantic pyramid scheme with him at the top. He had gotten quite good at it, and it worked surprisingly well, seducing quite a number of women from afar before ever meeting them, often during those periods where he was unable to get out and troll, using online dating sites as a venue. No longer a good-looking kid, he was now a handsome man, and he would come to spend his "adult" time in the company of some very attractive women, a lot of them, and for the most part, aside from what he chose to share with a couple of buddies, out of sight to anyone. To be sure people wondered about him, why they never saw an apparently eligible bachelor with anyone, but not caring what others thought, and having chosen long ago not to have a revolving door or parade of women through his child's life, he conducted his personal business as he saw fit, after all …there's a reason they call it a "private life."

It wasn't because she was the most attractive woman in that room, she wasn't …nor in his life for that matter, but for reasons he couldn't readily identify, and yet needed to, Rae Anne Johnston had raised a level of interest, excitement and questions that were all her own, the curiosity of which, the parameters, and the circumstances that had to potentially be navigated, and the big question of whether or not he would even attempt to breach the wall, were not easy questions to be answered. The dilemma occupied much of his time, until eventually deciding to reduce it to smaller tasks, not let his imagination get ahead of him as he was apt to do, and consequently prevent him from taking any action at all. He composed a note, waiting to see if in the interim she had given the meeting any thought, and what kind of response, if any, he would get. It read:

Hi Rae Anne :)

I've got a busy day, but I wanted to take the opportunity to drop you a line and tell you I was really glad to have met you. I've only begun to step out a bit this past year and already feel like I could write reviews for the local paper :)) Anyway, Leon's gets *** 's The crowd was mediocre and the DJ was okay, but I met a really attractive, intelligent and interesting woman there ;) so all was not lost. We are getting ready to start a full day of football, heading to the State game with friends and they're in the driveway honking ...so sorry to be brief. Again, it was a pleasure to meet you ...and I really hope to hear from you ;)

-Jake

It was not his usual overtly flirtatious composition, but this was not his usual audience, he sought to open a dialogue or communication and hopefully, if she participated in it, establish some baseline for expectations. He waited with an impatience that can best be described as that of a child on Christmas Eve waiting to see if the figurative bicycle, or PlayStation 3, etc. were going to be under the tree the next morning. Turning the volume up on the old secondhand computer upstairs so he could hear the proverbial bleep of incoming mail if he were elsewhere in the house, hurrying excitedly from wherever he was every time he did, and checking it routinely even when he hadn't. And then it came out of cyberspace…

It read:

And, it was nice to meet you as well. Life is full of wonderful surprises, the philosopher in me is always trying to figure it all out. However, my philosophies are changing quite a bit as I grow older and I've come to accept the chance of meeting someone interesting as a gift rather than a moral

dilemma. Am I correct in assuming you are divorced or going through a divorce? I am happily married (the second time) but much more realistic this time.

My children, 2 boys ages 12 and 10 from my first marriage, and my daughter 6, are the center of my universe. But now that they are all school age, I am filling the void in my day with charity work and attempts at rediscovering myself, separate from them. My husband has been very supportive, however, I am finding individuals that offer affirmation are a rare experience in my life. We should have lunch sometime. I suspect we have much in common, perhaps we have something to offer each other at this place in our lives. Looking forward to future correspondence.

Rae Anne

He read it over and over again, as simple and straightforward as it was, looking for meaning and innuendo, and it was there. He would immediately respond, but waited until the next day before sending it to avoid looking overly anxious, like he in actuality was. In a different time he would undoubtedly been diagnosed with ADHD, and as an adult, even in middle age, it had not really tempered itself, but mutated into more of an emotional variety of the condition that once he got such a thought in his head, he was consumed by it, distracted, irritable and impatient until it was either satisfied or razed.

He replied:

Hi Rae Anne,

Thanks for the note, I would now have to add "genuine" to the list of adjectives I used to describe you... I halfway didn't expect to hear from you. As for our day, State lost ...but life goes on :)) With respect to my status, I am happily divorced and have been for 6 years now. I have joint-custody of my 10 year-old son, who is my "raison d'etre," best friend and more. He is all the things a father wishes his son to be and in the process has served to make me a

better man, because as his role model I don't ever want to disappoint him... obviously he has learned patience, how to admit when you're wrong, and forgiveness in the process :)))...

As for my philosophies and political inclinations, I am quite liberal and open-minded and sense and hope that you are as well. I believe that everyone is entitled to believe and do what they please until it imposes on others' rights to do so. I originally attended a Division II College right after High School, but soon proved to be out of my league, and after majoring in girls and partying they asked me to leave after the second semester ...the nerve of them :)) Anyhow, as I think is typical, particularly with men, I found myself examining my situation and looking for ways to improve upon it after the divorce thing, went back to school part-time, and actually received my BA in Psychology online a couple of years ago. As of yet I have not put it to use, nor quite know what

I'd like to do in that regard but it was on my proverbial "bucket list" and the fact that I finished something was significant on its own.

I currently operate a small landscaping and lawn maintenance business and while the work is difficult, and the competition in this area a bit cutthroat, it affords me a great deal of flexibility and freedom in terms of schedule which has proven to be invaluable as a parent, and the autonomy suitable to my personality. I was an occupational pinball for a significant part of the past 2 decades before backing into this profession, having mown yards for years as a kid, it was something I did to supplement my income while working other jobs until it became more of a primary source of income, and I took the leap to entrepreneurship. It has been difficult at times, and probably represents the point in the marriage where my ex and I began to take different paths, but life is a river, and sometimes you go where you paddle, and

sometimes you go where the current takes you ...and we wound up at different places wanting, and expecting different things.

As for you ...among _other_ things, ;) I couldn't help but notice that you were married, so obviously you are the one with boundaries in your life, and therefore I will trust you to define what they are, but I am certainly interested in being your friend in whatever shape or capacity that may manifest itself. And "yes," lunch or something along those lines would be great. I look forward to hearing from you soon. Ciao,

-Jake

Like a mischievous schoolboy who hesitates that fraction of a second before he pulls the _fire alarm_, revisiting the list of potential consequences, and yet does so anyway, he hit "send." Not too forward, not too specific or presumptuous, the ball was in her court. "Game on" he thought, and well played. He found himself frighteningly intoxicated by it, the

46

possibilities, the minefield of circumstances, and the obvious question and uncertainty of what "it" was, but as if some dormant and unknown alter-ego had come to life, he honestly couldn't help himself.

CHAPTER 3

THE MECHANICAL RABBIT

Jake's contentment would be shallow and short-lived. Despite his self-proclaimed proficiency in writing such emails, he was also painfully aware that letters and emails are two-dimensional and subject to interpretation …and therefore misinterpretation. They don't allow for intonation, inflection, a wink or a smile that accompanies a thought, and the fact that she had not responded after a day, now two, left him thinking he had misgauged her and in the process scared her off. But then it came, and it was reciprocal, equally divulging in facts about her self and revealing more traces of her life, as it now existed, playful, heartfelt and honestly more flirtatious than his. He was surprised to say the least, and delighted, and in usual Jake fashion, read it to the point of memorization, scrutinizing it like an English professor for her choice of words and the message's cadence and rhythm, systematically dissecting it like an NSA cryptographer for hidden meaning and clues ...and the all important things not said.

Beyond the very obvious indications that she was smart, well read, educated, she revealed a sense of humor in her note and whatever it was about her that had first captured him, had begun to build upon itself. It was still all unsubstantiated speculation, they had not even "spoken" since that one occasion at the nightclub, but his imagination was about to shift into overdrive and unbuckled at that. It was all so very odd, at forty-five he had been around this metaphorical corner before and while he didn't know what lay around it on this occasion, he reminded himself of his natural tendencies and past experiences where that moment of expectations hadn't coincided with the realities of a situation. Fighting against the momentum he was prematurely building, he braked himself, "slowed his roll" so to speak around this figurative blind spot to avoid crashing head-on into unexpected, irreparable disappointment and humiliation ...or a husband as the case may be.

Her reply had intentionally been honest and revealing yet vague, she too was finding herself inexplicably attracted to, and comfortable with the perception she had of the man, and excited by the thought of him and who he might become in her life. Had she found that elusive but necessary accomplice to help her escape her doldrums while respecting her precious boundaries? That real life "imaginary" friend of the adult variety she was hoping for? She wasn't just corresponding with the man, but instead drawing a map of the maze that was her life, and leaving it to him to recognize it, and decide for himself if what was at the center of it was worth the effort of navigating the complexities. In a very clever way she would slowly provide him the pieces of puzzle that were her circumstance, and wait patiently to see if he could assemble them ...and he would, but what it represented was a bit abstract and open to interpretation. She would spell it all out in no uncertain terms when they were to eventually meet again. But that, like most everything else that would follow, would not happen at a pace to his liking.

His schedule was extremely predictable and flexible under most circumstances, notwithstanding the "unforeseens" that sometimes accompany being a single-parent. Hers on the other hand was apparently not, and they agreed to get together for a cup of coffee, etc., the middle of the week after next to *talk* as she put it, and would call or email to confirm later. It was a rather long time to wait for a simple get together he thought, and the sparse correspondence in the interim began to take on a "straight to the point," "sent from a blackberry" business tone and he wondered if perhaps he was being seduced into some ponzi scheme by an Amway MILF. It had all the components of an interview he thought. What the fuck? But he had already resolved himself to following through, and at least laying eyes on her again to make certain it hadn't just been the lighting in the club or the ale. Little did he know that in complying he had cleared an invisible hurdle and potential disqualifier as patience was a prerequisite for her prospective friends, and before the time arose she would reschedule at the last moment just to make certain of it for her own benefit.

Her life was alarmingly more busy and complicated than he first thought, though to be honest he really hadn't given it much thought. Thought or thinking weren't exactly leading the charge where she was concerned but "feelings" instead, and he had that luxury. His life was immeasurably unencumbered compared to hers. She was married to a Psychology professor, the fact that she was analyzing people and behavior was no coincidence, she hadn't married him out of some unabiding love but more accurately because he was stable, predictable, warm and faithful, in many respects the *anti*-Frank, and outwardly they made a logical couple ...even Frank thought so. The relationship was inherently symbiotic, each fulfilling some need of the other, and as part of the exchange she learned much from him, perhaps even surpassed his understanding and application of the science he taught in real life terms...or so she thought, and she surmised Jacob as being more than just the garden variety good guy.

His very apparent commitment to his son, honesty with respect to his past and his acceptance of his responsibility in the events leading to his divorce were attractive to her. Instead of promoting himself, he seemed more intent on acknowledging and professing his flaws and shortfalls, celebrating his failures and that was appealing to her. She felt some adjacency to his situation, the details of which were enormously different than hers, but his ownership and understanding of them and the way he presented them to her front and center, were shamelessly attractive. She took comfort in the fact that he had something to lose, someone to protect, and whose interests he would put before his own. It made the possibility that he would disrupt her domestic applecart less likely, and that common ground of emotional "mutually assured destruction," among other things she would discover that existed between them, would lend itself to an unpretentious, uninhibited, and gratifying relationship ...at first.

His father had died when he was nineteen, a heart attack in the backyard while pruning an apple tree. It was just a couple of months after his second cancer surgery, and his mother had rushed in the house in a panic shouting that something was wrong, without thinking he asked his girlfriend to call for help, but being just a mile and a half from the hospital, they would be twenty-three minutes in arriving, and in all likelihood twenty-two minutes late. He had seen CPR performed on television, but his attempt would be unfruitful, and the man he thought indestructible would die in his arms.

Life had caught him off balance in that moment, pulled the rug out from beneath him. They had not had that opportunity to get acquainted as men, beyond the relationship of father and son, and there had been disappointment and tension between them in the past months, his dismissal from school, other singularly unimportant but cumulative nonsense that had created some distance between them, unresolved father/son issues. And as only time would tell, his absence in Jake's life at that critical age would create a black hole filled with aimlessness, impetuous and self-destructive behavior, and a load of young man's foolish trouble would follow that despite the advice and efforts of friends and loved ones, he would never climb out of, only survive to emerge on the other side of so to speak.

His dad had left him with clues, basic tenets about manhood, clichés mostly, probably as his own father had done. Jacob had memorized them, and in his youth misunderstood them in some measure just as someone who is simply left with an instruction manual is sometimes apt to assemble things incorrectly first before putting it together right. In time he would put content with context, and take what he perceived the meaning to be to heart, and aspire to make the memory of the old man proud. The most basic rule he had been taught was that if something was worth doing, it was worth doing right. It naturally fed into his innate predisposition for perfection, and he took it to the extreme in his signature fashion, if he couldn't do it right, he wouldn't do it at all, and on those occasions where his efforts to do it right failed, well he failed "very well."

Like Newton's laws of motion, a body at rest will remain at rest ...a body in motion will remain in motion until acted upon by outside forces, his adult life was largely characterized by peaks and valleys, and great plateaus and piedmonts in between. Periods of great productivity and great periods of inactivity, periods where he seemed unstoppable, and conversely periods where he seemed immovable, and he was quite aware of it all, but felt like he was sitting behind the wheel of a car without the key, always in need of external circumstance or person to provide the impetus.

Impatience comes hand in hand with such an affliction, but like a mule that will sit in the field and take a beating rather than plod another step without getting the rest, the apple or water it desires, he had evolved into the sort of man that was resolved to do without when he couldn't have what he really wanted, and it made of him a strangely patient impatient man. At this juncture however he wasn't content to sit around waiting for Rae Anne Johnston's schedule to ease up, so he had to hit the pause button on what might be, and leave the frame frozen on the fact that he had met someone of great interest to him, but it was nothing more than that at the moment. And so he proceeded business as usual. All of the yards seeded for the season, and leaves largely under control he was about to hit the lull, it had been a reasonably profitable year despite the drought and he had prepared like a squirrel putting away nuts for a harsh winter, saving money for the off-season, and shifting gears toward a part-time gig he had as a paralegal/investigator for a Raleigh attorney.

Rhonda Gibson had been Jacob's paralegal studies instructor eleven years earlier. Young and just two years out of law school, she had opted to hang her own shingle as a full-service practitioner, but in the capital city attorneys outnumber pigeons, and as cutthroat as Jacob thought his line of work to be where everyone with a pickup truck and a lawnmower was trying to cut into his customer base, it was at least a straightforward trade. If you did good, dependable work it served as its own indisputable testament and reference, in fact, customer willing, you could even put a sign in their yard to that effect. The legal community however, despite the implication of fairness, could be deceptively unjust and mean, the kind of community that eats its young or starves them into submission.

Coming from rural eastern North Carolina, home to vinegar-based pork barbeque, tobacco, and perennial High School football powerhouses, she had pursued the career for all the right reasons, to help people, and fight the good fight. But it is a profession dependent upon relationships, relationships with other attorneys, DA's, law enforcement, judges, clerks, the list goes on and on, the necessary network as such resembling a spider web, and she would find herself initially an outcast of sorts, relegated to the quarters of ambulance chasers and courthouse-steps JD's hoping to be retained on the spot by some poor soul who had shown up without representation and in desperate need of it ...not unlike the day laborers Jake would sometimes employ, only better dressed.

It was not an uncommon situation it seems, but she had found herself there in part by her own doing, having declined some professional offers, spurned some romantic advances, and winning a couple of low profile cases against more established lawyers and firms with big reputations and long memories, and yet she remained inherently opposed to being part of that culture and struggled as a result.

It had not been easy, she had the crows' feet and invisible scars to prove it, but prideful and relentless, like the area she came from, she had eventually found a niche without compromising or conceding. They had met at the beginning of that journey when Rhonda was finding the going hard, and had taken the teaching job in the evenings to help make ends meet and pay off three years worth of debilitating law school loans. It was a time when Jake was feeling some self-imposed duress to transition from blue collar to white collar, but it was a "color" so to speak that didn't really look good on him. While he was bright, he was also restless and easily bored. Physical pursuits and the immediate gratification they brought suited him best, and he would convince himself that he could make the sort of living he wanted for himself using his back instead of his brain.

In the process however, the two would become friends, and Rhonda would handle Jake's divorce and custody cases. He would eventually come to work for her part-time in the capacity for which she had helped prepare him on an as-needed basis, and more regularly as he became available in the fall and winter months. While he wasn't a licensed Private Investigator, he could work under the purview of an attorney's guidance, and the similarities between the two, and their fondness for each other, strengthened both their relationships. He had found that as he had gotten older, the respective road of his life had narrowed to the point that he could only maintain a few close friendships, and Rhonda represented fifty percent of the population whose opinion he genuinely respected and whom he trusted. The other half of that equation was his longtime friend Harvey, or "Chunk" as he called him.

Harvey Childers was a chunk of a man, at 5ft 8" and 240 lbs he was almost unshaped, like a "chunk" and they had known each other for more than two decades. He had about ten different nicknames for Jake, randomly evoked irrespective of the situation as if he couldn't remember his best friend's name at times, and he could have hollered any one of them out at any place, at any time, and Jake, with the keenness of a Plott Hound would have recognized the origin and author often with accompanying chagrin. Chunk had been there to pick Jake's ass up off the ground, literally and figuratively, on numerous occasions, and Jake had regrettably once knocked Chunk on his. They had not always been best friends, but through a process of elimination called life, seemed to have merely outlasted the other contestants in that regard and as time went on they would come to have each other's back and keep each other's secrets.

It was called the Corner Bar, but ironically resided nowhere near a corner on an isolated patch of two-lane country road. The owner thought it gave it a neighborhood establishment type of feel, but truth was, she could have named it *Hades* and it would have had the same degree of success and clientele. He didn't frequent it often, it had an atmosphere of sadness, and was also unfairly popular with the Sheriff and State Troopers. Not as patrons of course, but as a source of revenue since there was only the one road, and it only ran two ways, it offered easy pickings. And with depressing regularity someone leaving the establishment was routinely found in the local biweekly newspaper police blotter. But Chunk and he were looking for a place to have a few cold ones, and the Corner was close, or close by "country" standards that is, which roughly translated to only 7-8 miles away.

There were all of about fifteen customers in the place, which meant it was about half full, but lo' and behold, one of them was Iris Vaughn, or Ivey as he knew her. She was the daughter of a county High School principal, and had babysat his son before, during, and after the divorce. He knew her family casually, had done some work for them planting some perennials and cut-leaf Japanese maples some time ago, and they were good people. He hadn't seen her in five or six years, she had to be at least mid-twenties now he thought, and she recognized him as soon as he came through the door, rushed over and gave him a hug and a peck like an old friend. She was cute, had been a High School cheerleader, but he had always known there was more to her than the "goody two shoes" outward appearance her parents demanded. He had found the occasional empty wine cooler and Salem Light menthols buried in his trash after her stints, but he also remembered babysitting with his sixteen year-old girlfriend once-upon-a-time, and there was never more than one or two on any occasion, so he hadn't made an issue of it, and she knew it.

Ivey had graduated High School and attended an all women's college in Raleigh, with the intention of becoming a teacher. Warm and nurturing, she seemed well suited for it, but after two years she quit school and changed course and began a pseudo-bohemian lifestyle by Raleigh standards for a couple of years, and even, unknown to her parents, had worked as an "exotic dancer" at an upscale club in Cary, N.C., for a time, which too, she seemed well suited for. He had always liked her, she wasn't the typical teenage cheerleader prototype robot, perpetually effervescent and all "OMG's, BFF's, LOL's," ...and drama. She was quiet and out of synch with it all, as if playing a necessary role or fulfilling a graduation requirement until she could walk across that stage, accept her diploma and close the curtain on that part of her life.

He couldn't help but appreciate that in the process she had definitely matured into a PYT, "pretty young thang," and while he didn't particularly like the phrase "old soul" because it conjured up connotations of sadness and "the party's over before it's even begun," she had a depth about her that was uncommon for a woman of twenty-five ...or whatever she was, just as he contrastingly had a great deal of the boy left in him for a man his age, and consequently, over the next couple of hours, and three or four beers, the gap between their ages and the distance between where they were in their respective lives seemed to dissipate until she was asking him if he could drive her home, feeling a little "wrecked" as she put it. *"Are you sure?"* he asked coyly, *"I'll confess I'm entertaining some impure thoughts,"* he added with a half smile and one eyebrow raised, buffering the statement as if joking in case it was not well received. She smiled and gently bumped him with her hip, *"I'd be disappointed if you weren't."*

She and her older sister, Rose, were named after her mother's favorite flowers, ironically, of the varieties he had planted around their yard. Her mother June, and her sisters April and May ...no joke, had been named after her grandmother's favorite months... The irony of the fact that he might now be heading down the garden path to pluck one of those said flowers, and plant something of his own did not escape him, and the paradox unnerved him a bit.

Chunk would take the diesel home after having educated some young bucks on the foosball table, and Jake would drive her decade old Honda Civic. The plan intentionally lacked some clarity it seemed, and she promptly asked if she could crash on his couch to avoid the inevitable frown and dismay that would await both of them at her parents' house, where she was visiting for the weekend. And he obliged, with increasingly cautious hopes, but no expectations. When they arrived, Chunk was out of sight, retired as he often did after such outings to the upstairs guestroom he frequented so much he called it his.

Jake fumbled halfheartedly with the sofa in an effort to give the appearance of being a gentleman despite hoping she would stop him, and then put on a CD he had burned of obscure alternative music he had compiled from TV show and movie soundtracks. She was again reminded of what she had always liked about him, while he had the weathered exterior of a career Marine or the Marlboro Man, he had somehow managed to grow older, but not old like so many men his age, and despite the gray in his dark hair, and the white in his goatee, the schoolgirl fascination had grown into a mutual lust for the evening. She kissed him, and it wasn't a peck this time. She tasted of cigarettes and bubblegum and smelled like the summer after his High School graduation, which smelled wonderfully alive and full of promise as though something life-changing and unforgettable could happen any second.

She stood there in his kitchen, her head tilted to the side as she pulled the barrettes from her hair and placed them on the counter, surprisingly clear eyed and focused for someone who claimed to be unable to drive only an hour earlier. They stood there in the surreality of the moment looking at each other, reflecting on what had so naturally just taken place, both recognizing the absurdity of it like some stereotypical midlife movie trailer playing in their collective mind's eye. To guys her age she was a late night booty call, a young woman with a questionable reputation, but to him she represented the innocence and glory of youth, and in the dim fluorescent light …a flickering reminder of his.

Make no mistake about it, this was the exception to the rule, and he was more than a bit self-conscious of it. He was always flirting with younger women reflexively, in the bars, the cashier at the grocery store, the store clerk at the mall, etc., and while they often played along in amusing fashion, he had the expectation of success and futility of a greyhound chasing the elusive *mechanical rabbit*, it just didn't happen. He saw this occasion for what it was, it couldn't exist outside the bubble they were cohabitating at the moment for countless reasons. He was aided by the fact that she had known him, been a witness to the warmth that existed between the father and his young child, and she was in need of some tenderness for a change, to feel like the prize, and not the consolation, and the obvious desire was written all over Jake's face.

He felt characteristically nervous, she was as cool as the other side of the pillow, "Dear God please forgive me for I am about to be a bad man," he thought to himself. She put her finger to his mouth to shush him as if she had heard something he hadn't even said, and then she simultaneously unbuttoned the top of her blouse with her left hand while unbuttoning his jeans and sliding her right around his waist and down the back of his pants until pinching his ass and pulling him toward her with a smile. *"Bet'cha didn't see this coming when you left the house tonight,"* she said, *"No ma'am, but I'd be lying if I said it hadn't danced across my mind,"* he replied, in barely more than a whisper.

She took him by the hand and led him through the hallways of his house to the bedroom as though he were the guest. The last time she had been there she had put his son to bed. He watched as she continued to undress, slowly revealing a large, tasteful tattoo of a vine, ivy of course, which grew out of the crease of her pelvis, twisting and turning up the right side of her body until arriving at, and half encircling her breast, the image unforgettable and ridiculously beautiful, recognizing he belonged in the picture about as much as a velvet Elvis among Rembrandts and Rubens, but not about to forfeit the opportunity.

He had found in his life there were those rare moments that you don't forget, the smell, the taste, the emotion, …the sensation of which all come flooding back to you as vivid as the moment in which they were lived, years, even decades later. Even rarer he had found was the awareness of such a moment when you were still in the midst of it, and he recognized this as such. He stalled, propped in the doorway committing every detail to memory, *"I'm in need of some affection."* she said, *"come to bed …and leave that light on."* He thought of what the woman he had met at Leon's, Rae Anne, had written in her email, of gifts and moral dilemma, of affirmation, and while he would later want to print up t-shirts commemorating the experience on some juvenile "reptilian part of the brain" level, he would keep the details of the evening largely to himself, carefully tucked away in that lockbox in his mind that each of us has where we keep such things, and take the memory out on those occasions when perhaps he didn't feel quite so good about his condition, because they were sure to arise. It was an experience that would have some significance for a number of reasons, none more important than the fact it would serve as a springboard for what was to follow, and the confidence it gave him would be very attractive and necessary.

Chunk, having been the first to bed, was the first to wake. *"What the hell happened here last night Snake?"* *"Did you clean up the house after we got home?"* Not knowing what he meant, Jake got up to see what he was talking about. Ivey had gone, but before doing so had cleaned up the kitchen and dining room. She had taken his phone, called her cell and saved her number in his, then sent him a text message which simply read ***"Thanks for the ride ;) ...Give me a call if I can return the favor :))"*** A yellow barrette lay next to it on the table as an intentional souvenir. *"Chunk, you'd have been proud of your boy last night,"* he muttered with a grin, *"I"* for Ivey. *"Huh,"* replied Harvey, *"have you seen my glasses?"*

CHAPTER 4

HEDERA HELIX

It had now been almost two weeks since she had met him on her evening out with the ladies, and it had been her hectic life as usual, in short, busy as a cat covering up shit. A plethora of children's activities, homework, art classes, piano lessons, gymnastics and the boys' athletic practices/games, the balance of mental and physical stimulation she sought for them ...and herself, and yet she still fulfilled her domestic obligations and had time for her pet projects, i.e., social and charitable outlets which satisfied the altruist in her upbringing.

She was amazingly organized. But her curiosity of him was front and center in her mind's spare time as she multi-tasked during that period. She was simply pragmatic, responsibilities came before pleasure, children's needs before hers, but that familiar primal itch so to speak was flaring up, and she had hopes, high hopes that this fellow Jake might be able to offer some help, and their meeting had been arranged.

She was not new to this, it was not her first drive-in movie so to speak, and she had been in the proverbial backseat before. It had only been a couple of times, but Rae had stepped outside her marriage to Glen in the past. Unlike this, they were not premeditated, but random hook-ups often with alcohol involved, those sinful grapes whispering in her ear "It's okay...nobody will know...you deserve this." While he offered much to her as a friend, husband, partner, even when he chose to as a lover, she was now a woman in her mid-thirties and sexually smoldering, hungering for oxygen and fuel to feed the fire, and for the life of him he could not see the smoke, or was deliberately looking the other way like a man who knows his roof needs tending, but lacks what it takes to remedy it.

She told herself that his ignorance or apathy of it gave her an out, a *reason*, though truth be told, it was more of an *excuse*, the difference being a reason is based in fact and an excuse is something we merely present as a reason when one doesn't exist, a lie of convenience we tell ourselves to disable the regret or remorse. How does one justify infidelity anyway? Perhaps we deny the promise of fidelity existed in the first place, or simply tell ourselves that the *intimate* details of the contract had been rendered "null and void" by "nonperformance." Who can say for certain, but she made it work for her, largely guilt-free, like "diet" adultery.

The human mind has a way of collaborating in such matters anyway, cataloging behaviors that make the wrong seem right, filed away in just the right category; one man's act of "murder" is another's "justifiable homicide;" one teenager's graffiti = "art," another's seen as unsightly "vandalism;" one spouse's "calculated act of betrayal" is another's "justifiable adultery," ...get it? The mind colors these acts in a way that makes them defensible and safe, so that we can get up in the morning and look at ourselves in the mirror without self-loathing ...and establishes the precedent necessary to any good defense, so that we may do them again if we want.

Semantics, perspective, or just plain old "puh-TAY-toe/puh-TAH-toe" nonsense that gives one permission to do the unacceptable and inappropriate in a selfish pursuit of happiness and help "mark time" as we serve our sentence, prisoner to our circumstances, without trying to escape them. And do so without the associated shame that a Baptist preacher's daughter might be inclined, predisposed, or obliged to feel. Call it the moral equivalent of the "Security System" sticker on the household window when there isn't one ...it's really just empty bullshit offering protection against ill feelings we might ought to have, a psychological self-defense mechanism which keeps us functioning.

Whatever you call it, she was good at it, her compartments had compartments like a Russian matryoshka doll. She would not have a simple dichotomy or duality to her personality, she would have a plurality of guises, like Sybil, only it wasn't a disorder but a gift, available on-demand and each was recognizably an aspect of her. Like the K-cars of the 80's the basic frame remained intact, only the details adapted and arranged to the performance she had planned or what the situation demanded of her, mother, daughter, friend, wife, MILF, surreptitious amateur porn-star, and while we all have them, and most of them are socially acceptable, she manipulated them with the coolness and skill of a serial killer ...or a D.C. politician. Always in control of it, like that careful *southern twang* of hers, she would be better at it than anyone Jake had ever met, except for himself of course.

On those occasions she had scratched her itch she had quelled it for a time, but it had always been done with a bit of trepidation and unavoidable stress about all in her life that was endangered in doing so, and consequently it had almost always been done less than satisfactorily, leaving something more to be desired, but done nonetheless. Perhaps because of the business with Frank, some trace of doubt and suspicion in her partner was always present which prohibited her from truly being comfortable, surrendering to the moment, and taking what she wanted from it.

Undoubtedly, because of Frank, she came to consider it a viable option to her predicament. To bridge the gaps in what her encounters had lacked, what she had conceptualized and sought was an ongoing relationship without expectations other than that of "no expectations." With passion but without emotion, "no-strings" except of the "tie me up" variety, and the all-important communication and familiarity lending itself to a mutually satisfying, and gratifying experience. Where each party would get something they couldn't get elsewhere, or were afraid to ask for. It seemed unrealistic, but she thought it tenable and sensed perhaps she had found a coconspirator in the form of this brown-eyed middle-aged single father. She would present it to him in a surprisingly frank and businesslike manner, and much like the interview it in fact was, in typical Rae Anne Johnston fashion, maintaining the final say over what if anything would happen, discerning whether or not Jake had the necessary credentials, was desirous of the "benefit package," and wanted the job. Her assessment of all these things would determine whether or not she would extend the actual offer.

Jake had been diagnosed with something akin to a heart-murmur or irregular heartbeat as a child, it was not of the life-threatening variety but was best explained as having too much adrenaline *per se*, or a faulty adrenaline switch, the result was that he always had what felt like a degree of constant "***static***" on the line like an overseas phone call, or an AM radio station, a metaphoric "ringing in the ears" which he became immune to over time. But under those circumstances that naturally create stress in each of us and the physiological response of "fight or flight" sets in, his body would overreact unnecessarily to inane situations and stimuli, as if Pavlov's dogs once conditioned to salivate at a bell began to salivate uncontrollably at a whisper, similarly he frequently felt nervous when there was no reason to be nervous. And it had made for a difficult life.

When you combine the physiological aspects of his reverberation with the self-consciousness that comes from an adolescent and pubescent period defined by isolation and hardship, it was a wonder he wasn't a virgin. It created for a terrible intersection of conflicting emotions when confronted with females he was attracted to, the excitement flipping the hair-trigger adrenaline switch and the exaggerated physical response telling him to run away from the thing his heart and mind told him to run toward. So when it was said he was nervous when he met Rae Anne that first evening, and that it was rare for him as an adult, it has to be understood in the context of his life, that the nervousness itself was not rare, but the degree of it most certainly was. And "yes," as strange as it may sound, he welcomed it, because it meant something extraordinary was at hand that would test and draw upon all of the aspects of his manhood to stand his ground.

Psychasthenia is a $10 word he learned in his Psychology studies which he understood to be associated with unwanted aspects of introversion. Encompassing various elements of neurotic behavior ...phobias, anxiety, compulsions, the beholder of which knows are irrational, but still can't help themselves. Now antiquated and seldom used, it has since been broken down into more specific and familiar diagnoses such as OCD, etc... But then again, this was his understanding of it and Psychology is an interpretive, abstract science, otherwise there would only be one theory, which wouldn't be a theory ...it would be a law. And he liked the sound of the word and interpreted it for his own purposes to explain his compulsive obsession with punctuality, and the stress not being on time created for him. Being allergic to stress he tried to avoid it as much as possible. He could tolerate tardiness in others, but being late intensified that ever-present *static* in him, and consequently he arrived at the park before her, or so he thought. At this point not entirely remembering what she looked like, and hoping he would recognize her and not be disappointed ...and vice versa.

He walked from the parking lot toward the opposing park benches, "chin up, chest out, eyes forward" as his father had taught him, with a slow measured gate of well earned natural swagger enhanced by the confidence his encounter with Ivey had left him with. He had the understanding that this was an audition, and he dressed in a casual fashion for which he was best suited, and what he thought she had found attractive in their initial meeting. Boot-cut jeans, a white button-down dress shirt, two buttons undone, sleeves slightly rolled, and the hem not tucked, wheat colored nubuck work boots. A day's worth of whiskers in addition to the groomed hair on his face, and a bit of gel in his thinning salt-and-peppered hair, because "the occasional wind was not his friend." He was unpretentiously vain, and hoped to give the impression that he was extremely interested, but not desperate, as if he was doing the sizing up like he had another interview later in the day.

Cut a bit from the same cloth it would seem, she had made certain to arrive early herself, and she watched from a safe distance with the interest of a voyeur who hopes to catch a glimpse of the unguarded man, leaving herself the option to abort if need be, after all, it was still in the conceptual phase, but she liked what she saw. She was reminded of a phrase her grandmother would use when her grandfather would strut around taking delight in surveying the 100+ acres of farmland they owned, the old woman chiding him lovingly about "priding around like a Bantam rooster," and in similarly appealing fashion, Jake strode up like the "cock of the walk" unaware of his audience, but much like she had been that first night, she was attracted to him, and the *relevant* humidity began rising between her stonewashed thighs.

It had been an unusually long time for a man with a short attention span, between point A: (Leon's) and now point B: (A small neighborhood park in west Raleigh). He had revisited the communications between them, and the absence of detail and brevity left him halfway expecting this woman to try and sell him some of her daughter's fundraiser cookies, or a year supply of toilet tissue. It seemed like he had met her a month ago, but only eleven days had passed and he needed to be reminded of why he was even there, but then he saw her, and all hell quietly broke loose within the man.

Only in North Carolina can it be 30° one day in November, and 70° the next. She sauntered up wearing a faded pair of vintage jeans, with the appropriate well-earned fray, an **Abercrombie & Fitch** t-shirt and one of her sons' baseball cap with a short ponytail pulled through the back, her brunette hair now shimmering with a hint of auburn, and no makeup, she didn't need it ...God help him. He would have probably agreed to murder for hire right then and there, figuratively of course, or at least offered up the contents of his wallet for the opportunity to unwrap her. He had the look on his face of a man about to go over the waterfall and knows there's nothing he can do to avoid it. Life had slowed such that seconds seemed like minutes. His sudden self-awareness of weakness where she was concerned, seemingly announced in his smiling eyes and bashful grin. If this doesn't work out I can always pursue stalking, he joked to himself.

Ivey who?   No disrespect intended, the young woman would have her well-deserved and rightfully distinguished place in that heart-shaped box of amorous events, but right now the name conjured up nothing more than the image of *Hedera Helix*, which was not a Cuban singer, but the scientific name for common English ivy as it was known at the plant nurseries he did business with ...something else he had planted with great success. The experience had been unbelievable, ***truly*** unbelievable, like a beautiful *mirage* unbelievable, but he was now staring at a potential *oasis*, which like one of those tricky damn SAT questions: **Reason is to Excuse as; A) Oasis is to Mirage...** i.e., one is real, the other is not, and he could only think about the possibility of the refreshment it might offer him if he played this right.

He rose to greet her, a simple handshake seemed formal and impolite but would have to suffice for now he decided in the half-second before things got awkward, after all they were in a public place, and at best like prison pen pals gathering to discuss ...her escape, a conjugal visit or what? She would resolve the dilemma, extending her hand first, with a *"Hey you, nice to see you again. I bet you forgot what I looked like, sorry to show up looking such a mess."* A darn hot mess he told himself, and like the night at the club, he felt himself slowly turning into Billy Bob Thornton in **Sling Blade**, as if he might start speaking in monosyllabic utterances about *"biscuits and mustard,"* and *"liking some French fried potaters,"* when she unfairly flashed that wicked grin, touched him on the hand, and fucked his head up momentarily.

Bypassing any small talk because her schedule didn't allow for it, she sat down across from him, her legs crossed, and seamlessly began to lay out her situation succinctly like a CEO who had a plane to catch. What was absent from her marriage, what wasn't, what she ideally wanted from him, what was acceptable/unacceptable, what he could expect in return, the deal and the deal-breakers so to speak. In short it sounded a lot like a sexual 401k plan to her marriage, to supplement the physical aspects. *"Are we good, what do ya think?"* *"Sound like something you'd be interested in?"*

Like any well-deserving applicant, he had some questions he had prepared for the "interview" regarding the nature of her marriage, i.e., was it "open," "polyamorous"...did they dress up like the butler and French maid and chase each other around the house, but she had essentially covered all of that, and all he could think to ask was *"Is your husband the jealous type? Does he own a gun?"* It was a genuine concern he thought considering his one past experience. *"No ...and no,"* she laughed. *"In fact I'm starting to believe he wouldn't notice you if you were sitting at the dinner table with us."*

Two barely acquainted strangers meeting like a cop and a confidential informant in the middle of the day to conspire to do naughty things with each other at the first available opportunity. This is great he thought, and incredibly bizarre, as in "too good to be true" bizarre ...I must be getting punk'd

…where's Ashton and the cameras? And then she pulled up the calendar on her smart-phone, and discussed availabilities with him. The weekend after Thanksgiving was open for her, the boys would be with Frank, Glen would be leaving for a conference at UVa, and Natalie at her parents. It was still two and a half weeks away and he didn't readily know what his schedule was like, he never had to plan that far ahead, but he would make sure it was open.

They dispensed with a small amount of chitchat, commented on the beautiful day, discussed how they would communicate in the interim regarding the details of the event, the possibility of changes as they always existed with her potential plans, and exchanged phone numbers. She wanted the option to speak when the opportunity arose. Did he have a girlfriend, was it okay for her to call, if so, when? *"No girlfriend, yes you can call, and anytime is fine, leave a message if I don't pick up."* was the response. It was okay for him to call as well, and she hoped he would, but she preferred a private or blocked number, <u>daytime</u> only during the week. And at this point, no texts since her kids often used her phone, beyond that email was still fine. He winked and nodded showing his understanding. He didn't need to take notes.

She gathered herself up, removed the hat, and stuffed it in her big Mommy purse she had brought which was big enough to hold all the things a mommy might need, as opposed to a "hoochie" purse the hoochies at the nightclubs carry, big enough for only the cash, ID's, cigarettes, and condoms, etc., they might require. She undid the ponytail and shook out her hair like Eva Longoria in one of those "Because I'm Worth It" shampoo commercials, told him to walk her to her Suburban, and the gentleman that he was followed suit. He opened the door for her, taking note of all the kids' stuff inside, and smiling at the all too familiar clutter.

He wanted to get inside and go with her. She gave him a hug like an old friend might, a hug that was publicly appropriate, and yet he still had to discreetly adjust his emerging member. They looked at each other with the intensity and curiosity that people must who are party to a mutually agreeable arranged marriage, or perhaps more accurately, like two strangers on the set of an amateur porn video awaiting their call to duty, "lights, camera, *FORNICATION*!!" Neither knowing quite what to expect, but the sexual tension increasingly apparent to them both. He thought himself to be fully capable of assisting her with her "needs," and she sensed it. Unless something unexpected came up, in little more than two weeks time they'd be "rubbing bellies" together.

CHAPTER 5

LOSE YOURSELF

He was a cute boy who had been disfigured by the mean-spirited intentions of an asshole older neighbor at the age of six, eating a fastball at close range, hit with the "ugly stick" so to speak, and he would endure five years of buckteeth before his parents discovered orthodontics, and another five years of braces. Time doesn't really heal all wounds, its more like a car rolling down the highway past a sign, as we glance back it simply occupies less and less of the landscape with distance, the indentations the wounds have made however are permanent, and sometimes even late in life, we still feel the pain, each of us merely children grown older.

At an age when children are perhaps their meanest, he was stuck in what seemed like a decade long game of tag, and was "it" the entire time. It is a time in our development when we are developing friendships and honing social skills, and he was emotionally relegated to standing with his nose in the corner, while others were recognizing aptitudes and abilities and defining their image of self, his image in the school picture was not the image of the cute boy it had been, and the internal disagreement between the innately confident kid, and the unattractive one in the mirror damaged him beyond his appearance and would have long lasting effects in terms of self-confidence years after these events were in the rearview mirror, out of the conscious and even subconscious mind, but weaved into the fiber of his being, the insecurities of the boy residing somewhere deep inside the man. It would make him more durable and empathetic though, what doesn't kill you makes you stronger ...or cripples you.

Those are the years that shape us. The clay of our DNA material sculpted into the raw form of the individuals we will be the rest of our lives, decide the paths available to us, reveal our natural predispositions, and affect how we will live our lives, the roads we will take, and how we feel about ourselves along the way. It wasn't fair, life isn't.

Good things happen to bad people, bad things happen to good people, but from sad beginnings come happy endings, or so the fortune cookie said, and that was his mantra. There is no doubt truth to the saying "Children learn what they live," and he had learned that while you can domesticate an animal, an element of the wild in the animal still remains, and in his teenage years, as the orthodontist's braces came off, so did the psychological restraints, and as biology continued its work he would leave the cage and go on a rampage, making up for lost time and refusing to be denied what he thought to be his rightful happiness, even if it required some occasional artificial assistance.

He met a girl, fell in love, and it had all the beauty and tenderness that a first love should, and as the song goes, "*The first cut is the deepest*." But he wound up being unfaithful to her, not because she wasn't all the things he wanted her to be, but because at that point in his life, all the pent up need for acceptance was more than he could strangle. His infidelity had unwittingly invited a stranger into the relationship, guilt. And guilt is a rude houseguest, while the young woman never expressed any knowledge of it, the secret created an invisible third party to the intimacy of their relationship that tortured him, and like an iceberg breaking apart from the glacier, he watched as she floated away, a young man's pride and the damn guilt prohibiting him from trying to stop her. But there's a reason they're called first loves, and that's because we usually have subsequent ones and this one left the watermark on his heart by which he would come to measure every other relationship he had. And while he would be aloof, he would never be unfaithful to a lover again.

He found himself to be the hedonistic pleasure-seeking monkey continually pushing the button for whatever it offered in that caveman mentality of "Pain BAD, Pleasure GOOOD," but he had grown up in a generation that was surrounded and defined by experimentation. And in that regard he was the rule and not the exception, at an early age he began to use drugs and alcohol. For a time they appeared to be the bridge between who he was and who he wanted to be, disabling his inhibitions, but he had not grown up in an environment of moderation, but one of extremes and like many such things, they were prone to abuse, and eventually, the things that gave him some strength and courage, became his kryptonite, not a remedy, but another source of woe, and trouble would find him frequently as a teenager and young man. He developed a reputation, and ironically was all at once the boy your mom warned you about, and yet the one she hoped you'd meet.

Labels were applied as is typical, but sometimes labeling individuals and behavior is inappropriate and ill-advised, as they can become a self-fulfilling prophecy, and it seemed the associations and negative connotations were ascribed to him by others so they could make sense of it in a safe, convenient way, when the truth was he was just a young man who came to the realization he had made some bad decisions as a kid, and decided it was not in his best interest to do so anymore. It worked for him. What more can you ask for? His relationship with his girlfriend was an unfortunate casualty of the period, and he left for Raleigh because he needed a place where people didn't have preconceived notions about him, and he could discover, if not reinvent himself.

At about the same time his ego and confidence would be slowly catching up to the strength and physical aspects of the man, the inside not yet matching the now handsome exterior, but he had begun to have some success romantically, and by the time he moved to Raleigh at the age of twenty-three, he didn't need to be too damn confident, women were beginning to present their intentions, and like a sisterhood of the falling pants, or pussy-mafia, they would make him offers "he could not refuse," and he didn't, like a malnourished dog prone to gorging when the opportunity presented itself and making up for lost time. In the scheme of things his game so to speak was that he was not a player, intelligence, a clever sense of humor, gentleness, and chameleon-like ability to adapt to the situation, his informal teammates. The shy self-conscious kid grew into the *ultimate boy-next-door experience* and an unassuming panty-dropping rainmaker, but as was to be expected the journey would be characterized by potholes, self-inflicted wounds, peaks and valleys, floods and droughts and long stretches of nothing in between, except his ever present passenger and companion ...the *static*.

There are probably two main reasons people undertake the study of psychology, first because they wish to diagnose and understand the things they don't like about themselves and rid themselves of them. Secondly, because they have a natural inclination towards it, the ability to read people and understand and recognize patterns of behavior and want to learn how to help people who need it, and he had done so for both reasons, but he had found at the conclusion of it that knowing where the stressors of his childhood had originated, didn't represent a solution. Knowing how you had gotten some place didn't change the fact you were still there, you need an exit strategy, or self-acceptance, and he would have to come to an agreement with himself, that he was who he was, and call it a truce ...start looking down the road, and not in the rearview.

By the time he had gotten to be forty-five he had slept with more women than he could recall, literally, he hadn't kept a running total, and to be honest their were periods in his life that he didn't remember all too well. But he had only had two committed relationships in his life, his first love, and his second, Rene. Beyond that, if you take a single man, and allow him to have sex with a different woman every 2-3 months over a twenty year period, well there you have it, they start to accumulate. And while he had long periods without any interaction, he was a hard worker of the grasshopper variety ...not the ant, accomplishing his feats in leaps and bounds, by the bushel and the peck, and simple as that it's not difficult to imagine, many just "last call" beauty queens ...but it had to be close to a hundred or more.

So many that the faces and recollections of the experiences were floating around loosely in the sexual library of his memory, their images occasionally popping up in his conscious mind, appearing like randomly drawn lottery balls, their names like newspaper word jumbles, when some song or circumstance summoned the memory of them, and he'd have to unscramble the letters to remember the names, sometimes going through the alphabet, **A, B, C, ...D**, "Deana, and her D-cups," and there was naturally a smaller contingent of women whose encounters he remembered for the animal-like attraction and the energy expended, women whose last names he didn't know, they bypassed going to the movies, or dinner, just straight to bed and exhaustingly scrogged like critters, they literally had nothing else in common except the fact they both knew what was going down the moment they met.

Aside from the rank and file of these partners there remained a higher echelon of women he couldn't forget, never far from the surface, a minority compared to the rest. Women who had emotion if not a level of love attached to their time in his life, the aforementioned pair and a dozen or so short-term relationships, women whom he had been upfront with about his nature, and what they could expect from him. And who were all initially agreeable for a time, perhaps because they felt they were capable of persuading him otherwise. But understandably, most women want to be somebody's someone, and he wouldn't blink at that inevitable dénouement. The relationship routinely souring like that carton of milk that had expired, and he would become the asshole that didn't show up at the picnic with her friends, the Holiday dinner with the family, or who simply stopped calling.

In a convoluted way he saw it as doing them a favor. Despite the abundance of good fortune he had enjoyed, he could more readily recall the names and faces of the opportunities missed, cursed with the reminder of the ones that were right before him that he had not pursued and wished he had. Forever "the glass is half full" optimist he thought, and yet discontented and fixated on trying to fill it.

His marriage stood as the sole attempt at a long-term relationship in his adult life, and after a few years he was realizing maybe it was unfair to the woman, the child that had grown accustomed to being isolated, became a solitary man, and while he would not cheat on his wife, he wouldn't have to. What remained wasn't enough for her to subsist on, and she would eventually grow tired and leave. But she had given him a son, and in time the boy would prove to be the anchor that kept him from floating away and ceasing to exist, and for that he would forever be grateful, and like the ties that bind, it would require them to remain friendly, if not at least civil.

At this point in his life he had the appearance of a Mickey Rourke-ish cad, somewhere between the **9 ½ Weeks** and **The Wrestler** visages, not literally of course, but he had maintained a very good physical specimen, not just for a man his age, but in general, however 20+ years of working outdoors had left him with a leathery complexion, and he looked his age. Nevertheless he had long since adopted the attitude "**I ain't good-looking but I ain't shy, ain't afraid to look a girl in the eye,**" from that Bob Seger tune. Though it was often accompanied by a degree of difficulty and verbal constipation in its application, he managed to articulate himself in a way that was foreign to his appearance and the contradiction of the man he was and the man he appeared to be was like catnip to the *kitties*. His accomplishments lent themselves to a well-earned confidence, and not its ugly cousin arrogance. He was remarkably humble and appreciative of every woman he'd "met." So to be clear, he was never the best looking man in any room, but he was often the most examined, and women found him sexy and *curious*, as if they couldn't decide if they wanted to sleep with him or not. And in that "hesitation kills the squirrel crossing the road" moment of indecision, he would take his best shot to get the *nut*, and succeeded with surprising regularity.

He understood his behavior wasn't normal, not in an aberrant way, but nothing to brag about. It was more aptly a sad reflection of the fact he had come to some acceptance that he was simply not of the monogamous variety, and had a strong aversion to the lies and drama that trying to pretend to be demanded. It was either that, or in a less flattering and more accurate sense, he just wasn't very good at relationships except those of the temporary and disposable variety. And relationships are work, and he either didn't have the energy for them, or the desire to be burdened with the associated responsibilities.

Whether by nature or nurture, he was definitely a bit of a stray, and one of the collateral side effects of his childhood was the fact that he had grown up to be a man who didn't require the constant company of others. He wasn't anti-social, he simply wasn't uncomfortable being alone, but he was definitely a sexual creature, and one of the nicknames that

Chunk had for him was Jake Dawg, and it fit like a collar. He came from a long line of prolific men, his grandfather and great-grandfather siring children well into their sixties at a time when the average lifespan of a man was probably forty-five, he almost seemed predisposed to an obsession with it.

So for better or worse, our boy Jake was a bit of a loner, and invariably for some, the hunt is more gratifying than the kill, the chase more exciting than the capture, the journey more enjoyable than the destination ...the kill, the capture, the destination offering mere evidence and validation of the pursuit, but once satisfied and accomplished we plan anew. Set out to hunt another trophy for the man-cave, and Rae Anne Johnston had that aura about her, and he was tragically *romantically dyslexic*, an overachiever constantly pursuing the unavailable and unobtainable women, or those simply beyond his level of attractiveness pay-grade and she was the ultimate representation of all the above...

In the sum of things, what would become so magnetic about her was that he could have her in all manners of lovingly sordid ways ...but he couldn't have her in the way he would come to desire her most, **entirely** ...she belonged to someone else. Like some obsession with capturing Sasquatch or the Loch Ness monster, it created a terrible paradox for the man, a seemingly endless, futile pursuit ...to "want" something he couldn't *have*, to "have" something he couldn't *keep*. It was an emotional cluster-fuck that would require him to prostitute his self-respect in an attempt to maintain some proximity to her ...like a drug addict, and make no mistake it pained him to do so.

If love is a drug, then *affairs* are its "crack," the excitement surrounding the illicit nature of it, the limited availability, the episodes and trysts characterized by periods of short intense highs and long periods of anxiousness and "jonesing" between fixes. And always on the clock, just as he imagined a crackhead to be, conscious of the fact it was going to end the moment it began, already thinking about the next time she would call. And as contrary to his code as it was, he would contort himself to maintain some value and utility in her life, and manipulate hers to keep others out of it. And just like an addiction, unhealthy, it would unavoidably have a negative impact on all other aspects of his life, and the decisions he would subsequently make. Not to state the obvious, but in some cases gettin' what you want ain't a good thing, and that reality would come to aggravate the situation and he'd find himself off the proverbial reservation. He would lose sight of who he was, and it would not be pretty for anyone concerned. But we're getting ahead of ourselves talking about something as if it's already happened ...like Wilfred Brimley narrating a movie.

Bottom line, the path he had taken to her doorstep, to this point in his life was about as crooked as a stick in water, and he thought he had a pretty good GPS of himself as a man, but he didn't know if he had taken the road less traveled to a common destination, or a common path and somehow arrived somewhere uniquely his own, but he felt at that moment, like he had wound up exactly where he was supposed to be. And while that's a whole lot of backtracking, and a bit of foretelling, it was necessary to say a little about where this was going for you to have an appreciation for where we are, and important to understanding the significance of the moment in his life, to this retelling of it, and essential to understanding where it would take the man as events unfolded.

He showed up characteristically punctual, his focus on the task before him made an excited determination of his usual nervousness, like a fullback preparing to punch it in the end zone for the go ahead touchdown with one second left on the game clock, or a fireman running into a building when everyone else is running out, the "*static*" was his friend on this occasion. He had danced this doorstep dance countless times, bedded more women than he could remember, but tonight was notably different for reasons he could not explain, he felt special, carefully chosen, as if **1**) Resume accepted; **2**) Interview concluded, and now; **3**) Hired to perform a very pleasurable service. And with the innocence of a schoolboy's desire to please, and the confidence of a well-traveled man, in the manner he'd become accustomed he was gonna "do it right," and in so doing exceed all expectations, including his own.

Like an overgrown teenager he had brought a mix-CD, yep, and Eminem's *"Lose Yourself"* was playing in his head as he walked to the door, it would have seemed terribly cliché if he'd had the opportunity to watch it unfold like a scene from a movie:

"If you had one shot, or one opportunity
To seize everything you ever wanted in one
moment
Would you capture it or just let it slip?"

But if it had been a movie, despite the dastardly nature of his visit, he was such an *"everyman"* there was a reasonable chance that the regular guys in the audience would have been quietly applauding him, while measuring their girlfriends' and wives' reactions with a heightened interest. Like a prizefighter marching to the ring with accompanying music to amp himself up, the song continued in his head...

"You better lose yourself in the music, the
moment
You own it, you better never let it go..."

"You only get one shot, do not miss your chance to blow
This opportunity comes once in a lifetime..."

He paused for a moment unnoticed, admiring the view as Rae sat visible through the door's window, a glass of wine atop the piano she sat playing, donning reading glasses ...as if it were even possible for him to turn back at this point:

"You can do anything you set your mind to man"

"But will I be able to live with myself afterwards?" He asked himself, "I think I won't be able to live with not finding out..." Then he rapped twice on the door, and waited for her to let him in, and just like that the guy you would've trusted with your wife and kids became the guy who stepped inside another man's house with bad intentions, and as all men are dogs of some fashion, in so doing he metaphorically cocked his leg to leave his scent, unaware in the process, his life would be fucked for the unforeseeable future.

105

It was a nice inconspicuous split-level home located about a mile from the campus, beyond the smaller homes, lower end apartments and boarding houses inhabited by long-time residents, students and TA's, equally close to the malls, downtown, the Country Club she had belonged to since her marriage to Frank …and far enough from her parent's home. He had entered a suburban *den of iniquity* for the evening and just as easily as he had wiped his feet at the door, he'd symbolically relieved himself of any suggestion of wrongdoing …and would never give it a second thought.

He had brought a six pack of Blue Moon Ale, having remembered her sipping on one that night at Leon's. It was a deviation from the domestic fare he was accustomed to, but he didn't want to show up empty-handed and thought it might be something she'd appreciate, and she did, flattered by his intent, and noticing the man's attention to detail. That *might* come in handy, she thought. She had purchased some Samuel Adams on his behalf, and aside from the initial couple they would consume as polite recipients of each other's gesture, they were both just props to the evening's entertainment.

Now we've seen how Jake's life could've brought him to this point in time, but how did the woman, a preacher's daughter, married with three young children arrive at this pivotal moment in her life? There are those ideas we all contemplate, for some they are fantasy, for others imaginary blueprints they have designed or stolen with the intent to use, carefully thought out to provide some escape when the time was right. You've heard that word "escape" a few times with respect to Rae Anne, and it needs to be understood that she was not looking to literally *escape*. She had a very comfortable situation, nice home, environment for the children, Frank's support and Glen's substantial income made it possible for her to stay home and be a Mom, she was immensely involved in all of the childrens' lives. It was all due to that firm foundation of family first that she had learned as a child, and a product of her pragmatism and organization. She had everything running like clockwork, and the escape she sought was obviously of a selfish variety and some would say, unseemly nature. To calculatingly plan to cheat, have another man in their home, and the events she saw happening would have made Jake blush, but she had it in her mind it was necessary to her serving out the rest of her supposed sentence, which she saw as the duration of three childhoods. And she had also arranged it her mind, with the distortion of a moral prism, that she deserved it.

While Jake had spent most of his adult life single, largely unattached and free to live his life as he wanted, she had been married for most of it. She had lived the childhood that was expected of her, and the typical teenage frolics and exploration most of her friends, most kids in general were experiencing, Rae hadn't gotten past second base, except for stealing third on a church camp outing. She had a sexual energy about her that would equal Jake's, and in a parallel, but entirely different way, she had not had the outlet for it either, and much like him, just because it wasn't tended to didn't mean it had gone away.

Quite the opposite, it had continued to grow, the desire, the need, she was literally burning from the inside out, and while she'd had a few dalliances as a young woman in that time prior to meeting Frank, she had never been promiscuous. It was almost unfathomable the self-restraint and discipline she had, and patient as a cicada. Frank for her was that step on the wild side, he was successful, attractive, popular, and an older married man, which presented an element of *taboo* which undoubtedly added to the lure. It seemed like the worst thing she had ever done was fall asleep during one of her father's sermons, and Frank was constantly throwing his attention and unmasked intentions towards her, discreetly of course. And she gave in to her desire for the first time in her life, and it probably would have ended with a fling if not for the pregnancy. And it grew from there, out of a *natural* Baptist necessity into a marriage. She had barely stepped on the proverbial dance floor so to speak, before the music had stopped.

Her parents were not happy about the way things had worked out, but if they had any disappointment in Rae they hid it. She and Frank had that chemistry necessary to a successful marriage, and if he had not fucked around *and got caught*, they might very well have still been married. She had that fire, and he was at least interested in trying to tend to it, and that was what she needed at the heart of it, some necessary attention, and an outlet. It was not a question of quantity but quality for her at that point in her life. And as our story evolves, Jake may well have been his own worst enemy where that was concerned. Even after the divorce she behaved conservatively in her sexual endeavors, she didn't have a husband, but she had two young boys, and they were the center of her world. A lot of women have a bad boy fantasy, and the preacher's daughter had a vivid one, but she found that the kind of men she was attracting weren't particularly interested in helping her raise her kids, and that quickly became a priority for her in finding a life-partner as she recognized the difficulty in doing it primarily alone presented ...and then she met Glen.

He was by no means the bad boy type, as the Docker's and Wallabees betrayed any intention he might've had of trying to present that *rebel with a pocket protector image*. And outside of the college community not a recognizable authority figure, and sadly she didn't find him all that sexually attractive. So "what the fuck?" you're saying, well, he was however brilliant, seemingly deep and insightful, and that had an intrinsic and compensating value for an equally intelligent woman, who at the time was in need of some guidance in things he knew much about, and she found his mind very attractive. But she couldn't fuck his mind, and his body seemed less interested and more uncooperative with time. It had to be the fact that she intimidated him. In a pragmatic, rational, *personal business* sense however, the man made a perfect choice for a husband, and she would be the one to suggest the idea, since he seemed to lack the initiative to do so.

They were married a year and a half when Natalie came along, and while she was an *unexpected* surprise to both, they delighted in the beautiful addition to the family. But theirs was never a love affair, it simply served a purpose in her life at the time. *"He was a wonderful husband...they were happily married..."* you begin to think that initial park bench portrayal should have come with "air quotes," a disclaimer, or some fine print that read:

"Wink* Wink* ...he's a <u>really</u> nice guy, and I truly care about him, but after I've raised these kids I'm gettin' the hell out of here!!"....

"In the meantime I've got an itch, can you scratch it for me? And would you please use your penis, thank you."

So there you have a picture to begin with, a hot thirty-something wife married to an average looking, academic nerdish fellow. We've all seen the couples and thought "Damn that dude must be hung like a mule," and he may well have been, but if so, it was apparently so big he couldn't produce enough blood to fill it... And it's doubtful that was actually the case as Jake would routinely hit bottom ...and he was not of the farm animal variety. It was initially that simple, which brings Rae to this evening's party for two. As noted in her first email to Jake, she was more *"realistic,"* about it this time, which now seemed an allusion to the fact she had fallen outside the marriage on two previous occasions, and was *realistically* intent on doing so again. And this represented a new endeavor for her, an attempt to cultivate an ongoing extra-marital sexual relationship, without baggage, unnecessary drama, built on a level of trust and communication, and no expectations or attachments... **Goddamn**, try saying that with a straight face... Friendship was not an integral part, only "friendliness," and she thought Jake the perfect man for the part, and he thought himself to be in agreement. But in the best laid plans of *vice and men*, things seldom go as planned, and as if he had instead brought a six-pack of *"I'm gonna fuck your brains out and ruin your life in the process,"* like some ill-constructed sexual Titanic on its maiden voyage, almost immediately …as if cosmically *synchronized* to do so, it would become much more complex.

She showed him around the house, a quick tour of the facilities, he taking note of all the surfaces, potential *points of entry*, and *impact zones* …and the exits. Like a contractor there to provide an estimate for a remodeling project, he was in that "I'm here to do work" frame of mind you remember. He glanced at the portraits atop the piano, beautiful kids, they all unmistakably had her eyes and smile. He imagined the boys looked like Frank …without make-up and camera lights, and Natalie, an adorably toothless blonde first-grader must have resembled Glen, whose picture he purposefully avoided as if like staring at the sun, it might cause him to go blind or worse …limp.

Like the dawg his friends purported him to be, he was already pissing in this one's yard, and about to steal his bone ...and bury one in his wife. And as wrong as he knew it to be, that thievery made the occasion more exciting, a stolen kiss better than a legal one, there's a reason they call it *"booty"* after all, right? And though she would need no additional allure for our lovable hound Jake, it had made her all the more coveted, like a pork chop. He thought the encounter with Ivey had seemed inappropriate, but it would now look comparatively innocent as if "sanctioned" by the church.

They put on the CD he had brought as they finished their beers in an effort to ease the tension, the anticipation had built over the past few weeks like that of the Super Bowl, the *Super Fuck*, it was surprising the neighbors couldn't sense it and were lining the street as he approached. You have to wonder whom they would have been cheering for, the ratio of gender preferences, and the reasoning behind their respective choices ...like a middle-aged *Twilight* adaptation: **Team Jake vs. Team Glen**. He was wearing his uniform ...you know, jeans, nice shirt, and those sharkskin boots ...what he thought any self-respecting gigolo or homewrecker might attire himself in. She wore an aqua blue silk shirt that made her green eyes even more unavoidably beautiful, jeans, and barefoot... Embellishing on it, he had pilfered a line from the film **Wild at Heart** and with awestruck sincerity told her "*You look hotter than Carolina asphalt in July.*" She smiled, "*I recognize that, shame on you ...it was Georgia asphalt,*" her accent nearly mimicking Laura Dern's character Lula. "*Yeah well, I guess you could say I collect phrases I think I'll have a need for, and I pocketed that one the moment I heard it, tried to make it a little my own, how'd I do?*" he replied, then not waiting for a response, with raised eyebrows and an unadulterated smile he continued, "*I've been waiting a long time to say that to a woman, I just didn't want to have to lie.*" She couldn't miss the intentionally unsubtle compliment, he was saying all the right things she thought, had someone given him a script?

The woman had a natural sensuality about her, and it fell off her like dew. She hadn't invited the man here to conversate, and she was duly becoming increasingly *hot* and *bothered,* and with a sweltering, purely southern sultriness, her lip curled a bit in that wicked grin, she replied, *"Talk like that could get you in some trouble."* And then she touched him, taking his hand in hers, as he then gently grabbed a handful of hair and slowly pulled her mouth to his, dragging his lips across hers, before stating with some clarity, but not boastful, as if it were a sudden awareness to himself as well, *"I should warn you, I'm the kind of man women fall in love with."* *"Unlikely,"* she replied. *"Only one way to find out,"* he followed as if thinking aloud. He felt the *static* coming on like a Mustang 5.0 engine somehow stuffed into a VW frame, vibrating like it was sitting at a stoplight, the adrenaline too much to throttle, but this was likely to get rambunctious, and it would be his ally tonight. Then the cute boy who had grown up with much love to give, kissed the pretty girl who had grown up with much need for it, and it was a kiss neither would forget.

They would have the stunned look of two people in one of those K-Y jelly INTENSE commercials when the night was through. There would not be an untouched surface in the house come morning, or suggestion of any sleep. He had outdone himself, and in the process of service delivery, the abundance of lust and attention had come wrapped in a genuinely loving fashion, and it had properly "fucked her head up." It was unclear whether she had forgotten what it felt like to be desired in such a way, or if she ever truly had been. But you can't fake that shit, some people live their whole lives and never have such an experience, and as a consequence, that fire was no longer smoldering, it was all ablaze. It's a wonder the neighbors didn't call for help.

They would replay the events again in surprisingly similar fashion the next night, this time at his place, And unlike **Holyfield-Tyson II: The Sound and the Fury** disappointment that Jake had spent $60 on PPV to watch Mike Tyson bite off part of Evander Holyfield's ear in the third round, disqualified, fight over, no refund. The second bout between our two participants was more epic than the first. And the end result was a resounding confirmation of what they both had felt, sequels to a great event seldom equal the first, but theirs did.

The coals and cinders of the weekend would burn in her memory for days afterward. He had abruptly made a mess of her little plan and dismissed all her considerations. Now she was addicted to the passion, and all she knew was that she couldn't get enough and wanted more. The emotional clutter and disarray he'd left behind after *wrecking* her notion of a sexual arrangement had blurred the picture, and she couldn't tell if she had *lost* herself or *found* herself in that two day window of her life. Maybe it's possible that in the "losing" we "find" our self. But *whatever* the case might've been, she was damn sure confused ...and he **was** not, and <u>that</u> would change the dynamic of things for a time to come.

CHAPTER 6

ADAM AND EVE

They hadn't invented sex, but they damn sure as shit felt like they had discovered how to use it properly. They would occupy a lot of each others thoughts in the coming days, and communicated frequently like two people who had been to an event like Woodstock or Live-Aid might to discuss the magnificence of the event, how great it had been, had changed theirs lives ...and that revisiting of it, the preoccupation and distraction it presented, made the daily duties their lives required difficult at times for both of them, and at the end of the day she went to bed with another man. It was testing that plurality of selves she had. There wasn't one prepared for this.

It had not been the actual sex that had busted her box wide open, it was the intimacy it had brought with it, this man was not simply a piece to the puzzle, he had brought several interesting pieces with him and it was unclear of the picture it would present. All the certainty that had governed and defined the plan of her life as she had it mapped out was called into question, it wasn't a feeling of guilt ...she had absolved herself of that before this began, but there was now an anxiety about her that wasn't there before, as if there had been some transference in the process of what he had felt most of his life. However slight the discernment or discrepancy, restlessness had now replaced her discontent, and she wanted to come out and play. In that fight or flight moment induced by her anxiety she would contemplate fleeing, actually leaving as in separation and divorce, all from the events of a single weekend, and not necessarily because the gravity of what had transpired was so great, though it was ...but because it had shined a great big fucking spotlight on what wasn't so great in her marriage. It would test Jake's resolve in all manners of ways as well.

Rae had the boundaries, and would need to be the one to initially jump the fence. She would find herself stealing away every opening her busy schedule permitted. He worked in Raleigh on a daily basis, and the opportunities therefore were numerous. It had spontaneously transitioned from a sexual arrangement into an intense invisible friendship, Rae was calling to see if he wanted to have lunch, a drink after his day's work, not for a quickie, but to simply see the man, and enjoy the way he looked at her.

She found herself telling him about her day, confiding in him in ways she did none of her girlfriends or husband, and quickly involving him in the details of her life, and "yes," marriage. And he listened, that was probably the most important thing he did. He didn't offer commentary or advice, but would simply listen. There was never an occasion that he didn't accommodate her, regardless of what he was doing, except where his child was concerned, he had essentially made himself available as if an on-call 24 hour service. He didn't do it out of some intense selflessness, but quite the opposite, out of an intense selfishness, and there would be those spontaneous trips from Franklin County to Raleigh as a reward.

There were of course those occasions when Glen wanted to have sex, and she would "oblige," because that's really what it was, obligatory, the performance of spousal duty. She had complained about a lack of it in the relationship, and consequently she couldn't really ignore it when it was presented, but she found herself thinking of Jake in the process, drawing comparisons between the chemistry they had, with that of her and Glen, and there was no comparison. She didn't start to repel his advances at that point nor ever did, not literally at least, but in that way that someone doesn't reach for your hand as you reach for theirs, or join you in the moment thus stymieing it, that was definitely going on. It had begun before she met Jake, and was part of how she was justifying her infidelity.

She had created a situation where the man didn't feel his advances welcomed, and then complain that there weren't any so that she could do what she wanted, incredibly conniving and effective. But he was more amorous than usual, probably because she was glowing, if human pheromones do exist she was exuding them and even he couldn't ignore it.

As the male of the species, Glen could sense that perhaps another dawg had been sniffing around, and men are territorial creatures, sometimes they want something just to keep someone else from having it.

So you've gathered from our story that Jake had been romantically claustrophobic in his post-divorce life, but this wasn't his usual relationship, this one had extreme complications, complications that conflictingly aroused him. He wasn't quite certain how he felt, but at least he wasn't in denial of it like some republican homophobe tapping shoes with the guy in the next stall at the rest stop. He had become involved with a married woman and was neither proud nor ashamed, but in a silent treaty between the two had come to an acceptance of it. And he was single, and she was sleeping with her husband, and the emotional inequity that presented for him demanded some necessary distractions to combat the feelings he was having.

Olivia was all of thirty-five, never married, in the fog of womanhood where she couldn't see what lay ahead of her, a period in life where a lot of women are sensitive and vulnerable about that uncertainty, and she attacked it straight forward with an almost antagonistic philosophy of a preemptive "shoot first, ask questions later" nature. She was extremely career-oriented, an accountant by profession for a local pharmaceutical manufacturer. Men go through a similar fog, only a little later in life, when the doctor says bend over and you have a different stunned expression on your face regarding a K-Y jelly experience.

She was an attractive African-American, stood about 5'2," petite, but stacked and didn't look her age, and was rightfully proud of it. She thought he looked out of place at the party, as if he had been called to fix something. *"Who are you?"* she asked as Jake stood shuffling through the host's CD selection for something out of the ordinary, he paused for a second, examining the interpersonal barometer for some indication of whether or not what he was thinking about saying was appropriate *...hesitation killed the damn squirrel h*e thought, *"It might be Baby Bear"* he chuckled.... *"Huh?"* she said. *"You know ...just right,"* he chuckled again. *"Damn... Do I look like Goldilocks? I thought it might be father time or dirty ol' bastard,"* she retorted, apparently hoping to retard his further advance, or at least insinuating she thought there would be one.

He had come to the gathering at the invitation of a younger fellow he partnered with from time to time on big jobs who had some landscaping equipment he didn't, and while not uncomfortable in any situation, he had spent most of the night inconspicuously tucked away watching as others made fools of themselves. But he was now up for a good debate, and without hesitation responded, *"Tell me you've had that fantasy?"* I can't be more than ten years older than her he reassured himself, I've got a woman her age pondering ruining her life on account of me, *"Don't be a hater,"* he said. *"What do you mean?"* as if her sense of open-mindedness offended. *"You know it's against the law to discriminate on account of age, besides, the older the oak, the harder the wood,"* ...oh God ...I did not just say that, he thought. Aside from sounding embarrassingly corny, he might need a pill if she called him out. But the banter continued, she'd pissed him off, and he'd intrigued her.

"*How'bout it? It's just one night, and you're not really my type either.*" In a carefully chosen chess move, thinking ahead, he had advertently turned the tables on her. "*You're a bit older than I'd prefer,*" he continued. "*I'd give you a heart attack*" she replied defensively. "*I have some aspirin in the truck and a will at home,*" he grinned looking her dead in the eye.

He had planted a cocoon of doubt in her confidence, and she would float around the party for a time apparently preoccupied with the turn the conversation had taken, watching with some disdain as he had drawn the attention of some other women, and it bothered her in some great detail, until it eventually evolved into a butterfly of challenge and curiosity, telling herself he had begun to take on a "*Californication,*" **Hank Moody** desirable cadness in the meantime. "Fuck him," she thought, as she then gathered her things ...and Jake ...and they took a Cardinal cab to her upscale midtown studio apartment nearby. It would be unclear as to "who showed who" what when it was all said and done. **"Oh shit,"** "*Oh yeah,*" **"Oh God,"** "*O-livia,*" "*O*" for Olivia it was.

Distraction aside, it was simply that, a one-night intermission to what was really foremost on his mind, and by now you would be justified in thinking our two contestants, Rae Anne and Jacob, had little else going on in their respective lives, but they did. He was now working with Rhonda part-time, and never missed a beat with his son and his active life, and still managing to get out like the single man he was. She was taking care of the house, her kids, her volunteer activities. It was all quite impressive. But the speed at which things were moving had left them both a little off balance. In little more than a month's time they had gone from a park bench conversation about a strictly sexual arrangement to something unexpectedly much more intense, and in the process there would be some collateral damage, the explosion of emotions proving to be too much for her *confined* space. Fortunately there was nobody in Jake's blast radius, but hers boiled over in a very loud display with Glen, but not an *argument* because he was not an active participant, but simply the object of her rile. After a few Manhattans with her girlfriend, she was more than a little inebriated and feeling a bit full of her self, the preacher's daughter's ego and libido inflated, as the attention from Jake had gone to her head. Not quite in a literal "*I got a man who likes me, na na na na nah nah...he thinks I'm sexy na na na na nah nah, he can't keep his hands off me ...na na na na nah nah, he put his pee-pee in me....*" not that forthcoming, but dangerously close, and almost as juvenile in tone.

Her words were like verbal pepper spray and a kick in the nuts, she seemed intent on emasculating him. The poor guy seemed confused as to what it was all about, and exactly what it was that he was guilty of, and apologizing all the while... He was obviously a very farsighted man, because it appeared he couldn't see what was happening right before him. It got so rowdy she related to Jake, that the kids were awakened crying at the spectacle of mommy drunk and yelling at Glen. A lamp was broken in the melee ...because she had fallen into it, and the old couple next door thought to call the cops. Not because they suspected Glen of anything violent, he was an extremely mild-mannered guy, but they thought perhaps some sort of Charles Manson home invasion might have been going on. The police would come, but no charges filed of course as Rae was nearly passed-out by the time they arrived and there was no evidence of violence, but police departments keep a record of all domestic disturbance calls so that officers show up with full knowledge of what they might encounter if ever called to that address again.

She explained it all to Jake with a sizable hangover the next day, and he listened... She told him she was thinking of asking Glen for a divorce, and he listened. She waited for some indication of his response to the idea, and he wasn't participating. He had told himself early on that he wasn't going to be that guy, which is so inherently fucked up and contradictory at this point. Told himself he would be the nail, but not the hammer, be the bullet but not the gun, as if one was less involved than the other, and he was trying desperately to remain true to that. Fuck her brains out, "yes," fuck her life up, "no." Mother fucker "yes," ...motherfucker "no." She would have to take that step by herself, if she took it he would be there to celebrate it with her, might be a contributing factor, but he would not be the cause. She had intimated to him she had some of these feelings beforehand, but Jake was not the *reason*, nor would he be an *excuse*. And once the hangover subsided, so did the emotions and the angst, she re-centered herself, took note of her comfortable life. Retreated to her original plan to see her children raised, and take care of her needs when the opportunities presented themselves, and got in the Suburban and took the kids to school Monday morning, then went to her pilates class at the Country Club, and that was the last of that. For a blink in time, she had come to the threshold, but she wasn't going to jump without someone there to catch her, and he had declined. She would have to make that decision on her own he told himself, without making more of a coconspirator of him than he'd already become. But in that blink she was there, and true to her character, it quickly passed, and Jake went back to being what he was always intended to be, her sexual 401k plan.

She found her way to Franklin County in the middle of the week, they both had openings in their schedule, and she needed some attention, and he felt like a drug dealer must feel when the supply has dried up and they have the only product in town.

She no sooner got in the door than they were doing it on the bedroom floor, she said she liked the traction it provided, and he was all about what she liked. It wasn't just that she would tell him what to do, what made it work is that she felt comfortable enough to tell him ...and he listened and didn't just grunt and nod obligingly, knowing that when he had finished his chores, she would ask him what he wanted ...and in time it would prove he had a lot on his mind. Men in general are essentially turnkey operations sexually ...no assembly required. Women on the other hand should come with instructions, or at least a paint-by-numbers scheme for doing the job right because each is different. He liked to be told what to do in that regard, not in a submissive way, but in a "Help me help you" way, it satisfied the "pleaser" in his perfectionist nature. And he would put the knowledge he acquired in the reference section of his sexual library, it made for a good resource, "The more you know..."

Sexual partners are like dance partners, and some of us tango together better than others, and women understand the fragility of the male ego, that's why there's the all too infamous "fake orgasm," but the flushness of her face wouldn't lie, and he had found there to be nothing so good for a man than mounting a willing woman, her kitty hungry for some meat, seeing the increasingly red glow about her cheeks, and hearing her call *his* name or God's. It certainly didn't happen every time, but when it did happen, it was better than an orgasm, and the effect much longer lasting. The "validation" that every man seeks, beyond the implications that **adequate** satisfies a *purpose*, to where **sufficient** satisfies a *need*. It was like one of those MasterCard commercials ..."priceless." More often than not men are likely to shoot par on the front nine, i.e., "36 strokes and goodnight Irene..." To be accurate, at thirty-seven she was a "do me" girl.... I'm lying here, *"now do me,"* not a particularly active participant, as opposed to Ivey for example, but the fact he was so attracted to her more than made up for it, her body an adult fun-park, the experience like having it closed for a private party for one.

He was flattered that she had gone to the trouble, made the time and the hour-and-a-half long roundtrip, and emotionally disarmed by her display of desire to be with him, and in the post coital silence of their play-date, as they lay there afterwards, he still above her, running his fingers through her auburn hair, it rolled off his tongue so naturally it seemed wrong not to say it. He told her he loved her. He had only said it to two women in his life, it had been said to him more often than that, and the absence of a response always signaled the death toll for those relationships. But on this instance it came out like a burp, unannounced, unexpected, and a surprise to him as well, not the feeling so much as the acknowledgment of it. He took the words seriously, knew the implications of it, the fact they had been spoken so unpremeditated wasn't a heat of the moment error but an indication of their sincerity, the realization of which had piled up in his head like an I-40 traffic jam at rush hour, and similarly bound to break loose at some point.

There is after all a reason they're called feelings, because we FEEL them, in the pounding in our chest, the trembling of a hand, a quiver of the lips, the body becomes electric ...they are not facts to be made sense of leading to a logical conclusion like some scripted connect the dots. Who in God's name would want such a predicament for himself? He remembered having seen a phrase on a sorority girl's Spring Formal t-shirt, it read: *"Le cœur a ses raisons, que la raison ne connaît point,"* which translated to "the heart has its reasons, which reason knows not at all." The fact that it took a 17th century French mathematician, physicist and philosopher, Blaise Pascal, to say it so succinctly should emphasize the poignant irony of it all.

"I love you too," she replied, as if a prepared statement of sorts because she had anticipated it at some point, recognizing she thought that he was a heart looking for a home, but she had no accommodations, no vacancy right now, and she continued, *"and part of me is really glad that you feel that way, yet another part worries that I may be a drag on you. I know I must sound happy and sad at the same time, don't think I'm thrilled at the prospects of you seeing other women but you're a lovely man with needs and I'm not going to be able to meet them all. Don't let me get in the way of you enjoying yourself with other women. We'll be friends as long as we care for each other's well being."*

He knew that everything before the word "but" in that statement didn't matter, and as he lay atop her it came out as if it was meant to be of some assurance to her that he was continuing his life. She had made the rules, he was only playing by them, and with an uncharacteristic stupidity he volunteered how he had hooked up with Olivia just that past weekend.

He had not even gotten off the girl, when like some scene from a movie where the alarm goes off and doors start shutting and gates emerge, he recognized as soon as the words were past his lips that the bloom had fallen off that delicate rose, note to self he thought ... "I just fucked my own goat." She lay there beneath him with her gaze frozen and the faux plastic smile reminiscent of the first runner-up in the beauty pageant, and he immediately felt the air coming out of her like a life-size doll from *Adam & Eve* at the announcement, she herself, stunned at the terrible revelation that perhaps her prepared statement had lacked some truthfulness in its entirety. Just like that, he had gone from helping her dig a tunnel out of her sexual doldrums, to digging a hole for himself.

He bookmarked the moment because he didn't want to repeat the mistake, but it was too late, it would come back to bite him in the ass. He had accidentally pulled a stick from Cupid's bag instead of an arrow, and she was about to beat him mercilessly with it, even if she were unaware of it. He had unintentionally stolen her "feel good," but stolen it nonetheless, the thing which he was the sole supplier of at the moment, the thing which had made him more than just a "fuck-buddy," and she would recognize the dependency and remedy it in short fashion, alleviate his propriety of it, diminishing his significance in her extramarital life for a time, and precipitously relieving him of his "feel good" in the process ...like a sexual pickpocket ...payback was indeed a bitch, and a fool and his heart are soon parted...

CHAPTER 7

ESCAPE

She had developed *feelings* of love for the man, and had thought of leaving her husband, but Jake, being true to his conviction wouldn't summon her out in an overtly divisive manner. She had crossed her own boundaries where the emotions were concerned and that realization scared her, especially when he was out there cattin' around. That awareness, and her *aversion* to it, undoubtedly represented the milepost where the trouble began. They had collided in a very intense sexual, emotional, almost spiritual way, and that was not conducive to her situation, so like the kid who owns the basketball everyone on the playground is playing with, and things were taking a direction she didn't like ...she took her *ball* and went elsewhere. This was supposed to be all about her and she had felt a twinge of jealousy from Jake's news of his encounter. And while she was relieved on some level to feel anything, as opposed to the comfortable numbness of her marriage, it was not the sort of feeling she was seeking here. It wasn't really a sexual jealousy, but she found herself *unusually* sensitive to the idea that he may be experiencing the intimacy with someone else. Women are often more affected by the intangibles partnered with sex and *carnal* desire than the physical act itself …and often less forgiving. The implications for attractiveness, desirability, and appreciation of their "gift" are deeply rooted yet easily disturbed. And that *twinge* had its casualty, the "utopian" perfection of their relationship had lasted about as long as a soap bubble blown from a child's plastic wand in a brier patch, and he seemed determined to reconstruct it …while she seemed intent on blowing some more.

In the meantime, there was actual life going on, Jake's mother had apparently suffered a stroke. She had been residing in an assisted living community in Raleigh for several years now, close enough that they could visit her often while she was carefully looked after, now in her eighties, in need of constant attention. They'd taken her to the hospital for testing and the results came back confirming that she had, and almost immediately things took a downward turn. She returned to the facility under the care of hospice. But the stroke had affected her memory and she now seemed trapped in a time warp, unaware of who was living or dead, or how she had even gotten to this place she had called home for the past four and a half years.

Perhaps it was a gift of sorts he thought, not unlike the childhood amnesia of the first few years of life that Nature so kindly endowed us with, so that we don't remember or bear the scars of that period of practice parenting, she was alleviated of the knowledge of her predicament it seemed. But he could tell she was frightened on a basic instinctual level, and he tried to comfort her as such. Who knows if in the end there is such a thing as *karma*, or just an individual's gasping last breath fear of it, of heaven or hell? The proverbial white light nothing more than the mind's screensaver, a product of untethered 1 & 0's bouncing across the mind's unconscious eye in random and meaningless order. No balancing of life's accounts ...and what if there were and you had lived your life in denial of its existence? He considered himself spiritual, but not religious, he believed there to be a higher power, he had looked at his son and thought how could there not be. Beyond that ...he was uncertain of anything.

Ann Fowler Arnett would have been a pageant queen in a different life, a could-a-been pinup doll in her time. Dark hair, green eyes, hour-glass figure, in many ways if like the song says, "I want a girl just like the girl, that married dear old Dad," she was a prototype for the women he was most attracted to, *minus* the neuroses. Life had treated her unkind as it often does, and in the process she had retreated from living a life to only living. Believing it seemed that if you did nothing, then nothing bad could happen. But that is never the case. You don't need to actively seek heartache and pain, nor can you hide from them. They eventually find each of us in their own due time.

She loved Ray Arnett, even when less of him came back to her from Normandy than left, and Ray would always be indebted to her, even when other necessities and ingredients of the marriage became absent, for her loyalty, he remained loyal to her. They were a product of a different generation, one that understood commitment, sacrifice, and had an appreciation for what you had, rather than bitterness about what you didn't, a "we" generation, not a "me" generation. It was also a harsh upbringing, and she would parent with that same degree of fear. As a child Jake had at times hated her, she could be mean, restrictive, and overprotective, while simultaneously neglectful. But as Jake had gotten older they had found the opportunity to enjoy a friendship, she had instilled in him a fierce loyalty and determination. And he would be there when she needed him, just as she had been for him, not always in the way he had hoped, but there nonetheless, irrespective of anything else going on between them.

Meanwhile Rae Anne was about to take a road trip. She had been asked to be the matron of honor in her cousin's wedding in Beaufort, North Carolina, a beautiful, quaint, historic coastal town. It was a trip that she would make alone as Glen was preparing for the start of the Spring semester. She told him she needed a bit of space and perspective from the frenzy that had been the previous month, and this provided a nice escape. She had intended to make a mini-vacation of it, staying a few days after the event, and therefore unlike the rest of the wedding party, she retained a room by herself elsewhere. The children's needs and business carefully arranged to be taken care of by her parents, Glen and Frank. It was a much needed and well-deserved break she professed, and Glen understood that it would be in his best interest to afford her the time. He might not have agreed with how she would spend it however.

She was going with the intention of having a fling while she was there. She would succeed. In the day or so following the wedding, when everyone else had gone back to their respective lives, she remained for a bit of rest and relaxation. She was feeling particularly stressed and needed time off from the constant demands of her life. Her husband agreed. She had thought for half a second to invite Jake, it presented a nice opportunity to have some fun without all the sneaking around, but that thought quickly vanished, as she reminded herself she needed a little diversity in her supplemental plan portfolio, it was too heavily invested in someone who had the ability to perhaps hurt her, and that was unacceptable.

She met Timothy at a seaside bar on a Sunday evening. He was there from out of town as well, a photographer and journalist from a travel magazine sent there to do a midwinter piece on the historic area. He was immediately attracted to her, and she to him. And after a couple of hours of verbal foreplay, making sure he wasn't married ...another disqualifier of hers, feeling him out for personal philosophies and how he might feel about her being married, he passed the entrance exam with flying colors. She would develop, or perhaps refine a sob story she had already perfected to the tune of *"I'm stuck in a marriage, my husband won't touch me, I'm on fire, I'm just looking to have some fun and broaden my horizons, I think I'm desirable...."* (fishing for a compliment) *"Why do you think he doesn't want to have sex with me?"* in that careful *southern twang* of hers. She knew she had the man on the hook an hour earlier, but she wanted to wrestle with him for a bit, reel him in, let him out, reel him back in so by the time they got back to his room he was ready to pounce. It was a delightful occasion, he was well equipped it would seem, and they spent the night together.

She had accomplished what she sought, gotten a bit of "strange," no-strings attached, and they would exchange email addresses as a means of staying in touch. That was important for her, for it to be meaningful to her partner, for him to have some awareness of the gift she had given him in the opportunity. Jake provided her that in abundance, she would find others to be less impressed, and less interested beyond the immediate gratification of sex, she was married after all. That limits the opportunities for a relationship to grow, and most men are not interested in such difficulties.

After the incident where the police had been called to the house, Jake had helped her set up a free email account over the phone while he was sitting at his son's basketball practice one evening, her husband was behaving understandably suspicious and she wanted a way to communicate with Jake openly, but without the worry, so he told her how. He had six different email addresses in fact, that was one way he segregated the women and his activities ...he walked her through the steps until she was finished, she narrating as she completed each step. Jake had

144

no idea at the time he was creating a pipeline for her to communicate with others as well.

She returned to Raleigh rested and rejuvenated, the attitude and appearance of someone who has just had an hour long deep-tissue massage, refreshed and relaxed. She had not had an orgasm, the familiarity with the man wasn't there, and neither was the level of comfort she preferred. She enjoyed controlling the environment, which was why she had been so bold as to invite Jake to her home for their first get together, and this excursion didn't allow her to do so. While she hadn't gotten her "O," she delighted in the fact she had given Timothy several, and in that there was an enormous affirmation for her, her desirability, her prowess, and it had scratched her itch. The spontaneity adding to the excitement, and it would become an aspect of her future outings. She called Jake and asked if he'd like to meet her for coffee the middle of the week, and as always, he arranged his schedule to accommodate her. It had been now three weeks since he had seen her, and he was anxious at the thought of how they'd left things last time, she seemed a little "deflated."

He gave her a strong but gentle hug when she arrived, and a signature kiss on the neck, again it seemed appropriate for a public display of affection, however she was not quite as warm in her embrace. He would later begin to think of how she must dismiss Glen in such a way. It sucked. They each sat down and ordered a sandwich, he a cappuccino, and she a coffee, black, no sugar. They had not been there five minutes when she told him she had something she had been dying to tell him, almost giddy with it, her lip squinched up to her nose like Elizabeth Montgomery in **Bewitched**, (younger audience please check **TV Land** for times and listings) he perked up eager to hear what she had to share, it must be something good he thought.

And then she proceeded to tell him about the guy she had met, how she had seduced him in a fashion, going into great detail in some *uncomfortable* aspects for our man Jake, and she continued to the apparent point of the story, and their occasion for this meeting it would seem, as she announced with great pleasure how she had come to realize through the experience, that Jake was not the source of her "feel good," that it wasn't specific to him, and she did so with the coldest satisfaction, like one of those guests on **Maury Povich** where the patented response was "You are **NOT** the father," ...she had declared he was **NOT** the source of her recent happiness, and she couldn't wait to tell him. *Ouch*, ...that *kinda* hurt ...unnecessarily so, and extremely uncalled for he thought silently, as he sat there across from her smiling, continuing his silent conversation with himself, *"That's great, tell me all about it,"* he replied and proceeded to listen, only this time he had the frozen expression of a mannequin... *"Touché* Jake... I'll see your bursting my little bubble, and beat you with this metaphoric club you provided me with," ...*or so it had to seem.*

He had never taken part in anything like it. Perhaps relationships weren't his forte after all, at least not relationships of this nature. It would get exponentially worse. He thought he had attached his heart to an unavailable woman, he had seemingly hitched it to Halley's Comet, and it wasn't going to be back for another 75-76 years or so it felt. What the fuck? And like Bob from the local morning radio **Showgram** was always saying, *"I quit this bitch,"* he thought. See ya!!!

You have to remember he had a kind of emotional OCD, and this shit was eating him up from the inside out. He could've hurt somebody. He went home and composed a very pointed and targeted email, of the *"fuck you very much"* variety after he had some difficulty digesting his "lunch," for it had not settled well.

So brace yourself, might want to go get a drink or a snack cause this could take awhile, but its relevant for a couple of reasons. First, it was impressive how the landscaper could articulate himself, and if you pay attention, he'll tell you in a sense how things could take the turn they did. Secondly he was a wordsmith, it was his **twelve-inch cock** so to speak, and he would poke her with it just often enough that she wouldn't forget it. The only common denominator between her "types" was that they had to be able to carry on an intelligent conversation, and he had no equal in that arena.

The first letter is extremely honest, it tells you what was going on inside the man, and in a sense it represents the last we'll see of rational thinking where she was concerned. But she would never see

148

it, there's certain to be irony in that. For the most part everything afterwards would be written with ulterior motives, so here it went,

It read:

Dear Rae,

You asked me to trust my instincts and intuition and as such, I'm sensing a change in the role I've played in your life, or perhaps sadly, a cessation of it. I'm glad you've begun your journey anew, and I hope time and reflection will tell what a happy, enlightening, and fulfilling one it has been. I also hope you find something to sustain you along the way. It is becoming apparent why I was brought into your life, to fan the fire, as a bridge from one part of your life to the next, or maybe just as a short chapter in the story you will tell of your life. We existed in a vacuum of sorts for a moment in time, and it was an extremely intense, passionate and loving period. I ache at the thought that it is

coming to a close, but I'm thankful for the experience of it at this time in my life nonetheless. I hope you have some similar feelings.

It was difficult at times to be separated from you, extremely difficult, and I think I could have sustained it. But I realized some things about your feelings toward me after the Beaufort trip, ...as did you :)) when you explained that you had come to the realization that you could feel whatever it was you felt in your experience with me... without me, ...and that I was not the source of it. And while I understand what you meant it was saddening to hear it, because what I have felt when I was with you was unique and specific to you, rare and not commonplace. The language you had used in the previous weeks is missing from your messages of late... *"that you could not imagine seeing me and not wanting to have a physically intimate relationship,"* that you were afraid if you let yourself you would *"consume"* me, *"the affection between us was so strong it couldn't be hidden,*" and that your "*insides were raging,*" that you had never met anyone like me, and didn't want me to not be a part of your life.

They are all wonderful things that will echo in my heart and head I am sure. But unfortunately they didn't really withstand the first pierce to the armor, and I think I will consequently have some doubt regarding their strength and sincerity, not to mention my ability to trust my intuition in such matters. I am glad that I have given you something in our friendship that was of value to you, glad that I helped push open that door to the powerful love we all deserve and desire, and yes, truly saddened, in the deepest of ways, that I will not be the one who gets to walk through it. I have shared things with you that I have learned on my journey, words that have a pain associated with them for me, and while I know you understand the meaning in them, they will never truly mean what they should until you too have a pain associated with them to understand their value and wisdom.

Thank you for letting me be a part of your life, for allowing me to travel however briefly a part of this road with you. In reality it will be a journey that you must take alone, and I wish you all the best from the bottom of my heart, and wish for your safety as well. You will always be the "third" woman I have loved in my life, and I will remember you every time the wind blows through the hole left in my heart of that space only you have occupied. As always...

Love,

-Jake

...and he promptly sent it without hesitation ...and then panicked as soon as he had done so, wishing he could undo it, to the point he began trying to access her email that he had helped her set up in an attempt to permanently delete it before she read it. If he couldn't guess the password he was prepared to try and answer the secret question to reset it, even though it would send up a red flag to her in doing so …he didn't care. His attempts failed to the point it triggered the automated prompt to reset the password via the secret question.

He had six adolescent boys downstairs making all the ruckus in the world, all calling for his attention and presence, and he was upstairs panicking like he had hit the launch codes for a nuclear attack, or the drug addict who in a moment of dread over their situation has flushed the remainder of their stash, only to then try and stop it from going completely down the toilet and salvage some trace of it, regretting the decision …it would have been pitiful to watch, he really was an inherently good guy, but unknown to anyone he was becoming an aberration of himself.

The secret question was *"What was your first car?"* He knew this, he had replayed the conversation in his mind, they were lying in his bed that Sunday morning the first weekend they had spent together, revealing bits and pieces of each other as unacquainted lovers do, and she had told him about how she was the first of her girlfriends to get a car. Her father was getting a new one and handed it down to her, it was a yellow Lincoln Continental, big as a damn classroom he remembered kidding her. She had told him that all the boys called them the 'Nental chicks as they drove around their Five Points neighborhood. It was so big they made her get two parking permits to park in the Broughton High lot. She kept it throughout her college years.

It was *"**Continental,**"* so he knew the answer to her secret question, but it was his last resort. He closed out of the webmail, and decided he would wait a few minutes, clear his thoughts ...and the cache on his computer, and try the password again, he didn't want to alarm her that it had been compromised if at all possible, and in the process close the window of communication. He pulled up the email login again, and tried a couple of more passwords, he remembered vividly the context of the conversation they had when she was setting it up, the password had to be something relevant to **their** situation, and what it represented to her, **escape** seemed relevant. He tried it, and boom ...he was in.

It sounds unbelievable, but it happened, and there he was in her email account, but there was a lot of damn mail and it wasn't all his. It was like a perverse soap opera, he was reading her emails from this guy Timothy she had told him about, emails from men who wanted to sleep with her, men she wanted to sleep with, and the competition was fierce and there was woefully plenty of it. She was like the cheese in a room full of hungry rats, and everyone wanted a *piece*. It would prove to be painfully masochistic to the pleasure-seeking monkey in Jake. But there was no going back, no erasing the knowledge of it. He copied all the emails and addresses, and everything that was saved in her sent and inbox and pasted them into a word document on his computer, then saved all the emails "keep as new" or "unfucking read," or whichever way he'd found them, deleted any trace of the email he had sent and logged out.

He had seen behind the curtain and the image had disturbed him. He had that summer camp "I wanna go home," look about him. Yet in spite of everything, he wasn't able to walk away from the relationship, couldn't change how he felt about her.

Unable to exit or make a U-turn at this pivotal point, he became that *crooked man that walked a crooked mile,* and this milepost on the journey represents the point where the man went from being *"different,"* to being *"weird."* From being the man he was …to some corrupted version of himself.

He would wait a day or two before composing an upbeat email that he thought would speak well for him as a progressive open-minded man… Written in a tone she would appreciate, surprise her, and hopefully alleviate any stress she had regarding his reaction to what she had said. This one read:

Hey Doll,

I know I probably seemed a little weird after the news of your Beaufort trip, and yes I was a bit jealous, but it wasn't necessarily what you may have thought. Contradictions are fine, even attractive... I have plenty myself, but inconsistencies are scary. I was still on the 8th or 9th floor of a 10 story emotional building and your elevator seemed to be falling fast ;))

Hell, if you recall when I spoke to you that Saturday while you were at the wedding you told me that you didn't want to have to choose between me and your husband, ...those are powerful, endearing words Rae, and in a day's time, or a chance encounter, all of that seemed to have changed. Perhaps you can't understand or empathize how the loss of significance (or the *appearance* of significance) affected me, but I hope you'll accept that's how I felt. The only possible conclusions I could draw weren't very comfortable ones.

Let's face it, for all of my experience and maturity, I've never been in a relationship quite like this, and I'm still feeling my way around a bit. I've had time to trim my sails and adjust my course so that I don't end up in the emotional rocks so to speak ;) Truthfully, I had to dial down the emotions a bit, and that's okay. I like to think that friendships are living things, kind of like a tree, and during the life of ours we will have different seasons, all the while the roots

157

growing deeper and stronger, and while each season will have its own intensity and passion (or lack of) it will eventually fade into the next, never gone, just waiting to evolve and return anew.

I hope these words find a home in your heart in a way which you find attractive, they are after all, a part of me which belongs to you ...whether you want it or not :)) So feel free to tell me, as always, whatever you want to, or don't tell me if that's what you prefer. I understand your situation and circumstances, and I also understand my place in your life, perhaps better now than before.

As you know ...or are learning, I am not one to refrain from saying what I feel... I think it's emotionally unhealthy to do so, and I needed for you to know this because I've sensed a degree of awkwardness that doesn't need to be there. And look, if I've misinterpreted something on your behalf, you need to let me know.

Sorry I haven't written before now. I enjoy getting emails from you as often as you can write, and you can always expect to get them back from me. Those days when I check my email and find one from you are always better than the ones I don't ;) I look forward to seeing you ...in any capacity, soon :)) Call or write. As always...

Love,

-Jake

She would reply:

I wanted to cry after reading your letter. Nothing you said surprises me. You are right when you say I am not immune to jealously. Perhaps I was being a bit manipulative. I don't know how to begin to respond to such a thoughtful message but I'll try. First, I think you are an incredibly wonderful person because you do tell me what you are thinking and feeling. I find this very attractive about you among other things. I don't mean to be inconsistent although I have been all that and more in the last few weeks. Let's face it I am a very confused individual on many levels and yet solid as a rock on others, and I am having all kinds of positive and negative feelings.

The bottom line for me is that I have so many desires and opposing concerns, and anything I THINK threatens or adds to them scares me away a bit. I really do care for you and part of me thinks that I could really get caught up in this relationship, and "yes," that frightens me Jake, so I keep all doors open because I'm going to be here for a while to come. Is that a contradiction? Absolutely. You'll have to decide if this relationship is worth the pain it may inflict. I hope you know my thoughts on that. I will talk to you soon.

Love,

Raen

It was the first time she had used her nickname, afforded him access to that layer of herself, it was significant, or intentionally meant to seem so, who knows? Her post coitus this time would leave her feeling a bit depressed after the endorphins had retreated. She actually felt as if she had cheated on two men, her husband <u>and</u> Jake, and she was in all likelihood more regretful of the latter.

It was wrong, he knew it, and it was so wrong he wouldn't tell anyone, and as a result he would definitely lose his bearings for a time. He felt like that tractor trailer we've all seen on the highway, out of align, his ass-end swaying, not following the front. His actions about to change lanes against the advice and logic of his mind, his instincts telling him to *abort ...abandon ship ...run like hell!!!* But he couldn't help it, sad as it was, there is no reasoning with emotions remember, so with an eye towards regaining the upper hand, like a bully on an invisible playground he was going to have to create some apprehension and doubt about her other options ...until like it or not, he was the only playmate available.

He was like a drug dealer in a sense. Trying to eliminate the competition to monopolize the supply of what she sought, all the while simultaneously and surreptitiously telling her what she sought ...**him**. And to accomplish that he came up with an idea he thought would put a hitch in her giddy-up, the "fear of God" in her horny ass, and it went something like this:

The summer before he moved to Raleigh, he had slept with a friend's ex-girlfriend, who just happened to be his ex-girlfriend's best friend ...even at the time it seemed incestuous and a very perverted killing of two birds with one stone. Blame it on Rio, or in this case chalk it up to Myrtle Beach, and as Mark Twain said "Of all the things I've lost, I miss my mind the most." There must be one helluva cerebral *Lost and Found* in Horry County South Carolina...

In the aftermath of the encounter, in typical hypochondriac fashion or perhaps simply erroneously guilt ridden, he convinced himself he had contracted an STD. Obsessed and fixated on the possibility, he went to the county health clinic and got checked. The test came back negative, but he had persistent *symptoms* so the physician gave him a prescription for an antibiotic just in case he had a dose of chlamydia which isn't easily diagnosed ...and much more likely because he recognized it was probably the only cure for the young man's very *diagnosable* case of anxiety regarding it.

It had slowed his roll to be sure, and Jake wasn't above using the reincarnation of such an experience as a deterrent where Rae was concerned. He knew that despite whatever precautions the woman had taken, she couldn't help but be alarmed at the suggestion she had contracted something in her excursion and given it to him, or worse yet ...her breadwinner.

He waited a painfully long and difficult period of time for an impatient man before responding, which *roughly* translated to about a week. His intention being to take the intensity level down a bit, give her time to think about things, and then follow up with another novella, putting her mind at ease and taking a step toward coaxing her into coming out to play so the story had some logic and bite to it. It's hard to catch a Sexually Transmitted Disease <u>without</u> the Sex. It was wrong on any number of levels, but fear can be a great means of discouraging *undesirable* behavior, at least in the <u>short-term</u>, and in his harried state of mind, the *"end"* justified the *"means."* It read:

Rae,

If you reread some of the emails I have sent you over the course of our correspondence you will find pieces of the sort of man I am... If I can't have what I want, I'll do without ...sex is great, sex with emotions is amplified ...a little bit of meaningful sex is better than a lot of meaningless. Don't feel anything other than happy that I feel the way I do, it doesn't mean I will do without anything. It is as I told you before, I have the right to do what I want ...and the right not to do what I don't want to do. As for me, I continue to explore every option available to me, though I did cease looking for a time. And I don't feel compelled to tell

you everything that I do. I realized early on that sometimes its serves no good purpose to invite others into a relationship, for example that Wednesday that you came to see me after you had the big argument, and we were on the floor and I blurted out at an inopportune moment that I'd had sex with another woman that weekend, I noticed something wash across your face. It seemed as if your "feel good" had essentially left the room, and consequently I have refrained from telling you about any sexual encounters I've had since, because as you once said, we will be friends for as long as we care about each other's well-being.

I haven't decided whether or not I want to know about everyone you have sex with, is that a requirement implicit of me, does it make me less attractive, or is it not enough that I don't care what you do? I don't know how I feel about it. In reality that could become a bed so crowded it doesn't have room for real intimacy because of all the "ghosts." Most men will either offer you freedom, or their love, the two of them are mutually exclusive for the majority of people. I have tried to offer you both, perhaps unsuccessfully ...only you know for certain. In any respect, questions of pain and hurt have no place here, they are two-way streets that are inherent in any relationship, and we passed that exit. But I appreciate your concern in that regard.

In truth, if our friendship has any enduring aspects or longevity, as we both once said we believe it to, it will be because of how we have cared about each other, and little else. My only intention in writing that last letter was to correct any misconceptions you may have had regarding where my head/heart were at, and to eradicate any awkwardness. With that in mind why would a healthy red-blooded man like myself want to close the door on having an occasional tryst with a woman I have always found attractive?

For whatever reason, a number of very desirable women are making themselves available to me. Some have theirs claws visible, others ...their intentions remain unclear. A couple of months ago, I might have been scrambling and clamoring to bed them all, but now I stand back, satiated from my experience with you rather like a fat man at a buffet, carefully choosing which dessert I will take, if any, rather than needing them all. Even though I may eventually choose them all ;))

You were telling me of all the offers that were on your table (from other men) and I know I might not have reacted as you might have wished with the news of your adventure. But that's where I'm at with it, and I reserve the right to be honest. I'm apparently a little jealous, I'm not proud of it, the emotion is foreign to me, but its there. I think if I weren't it would mean I didn't care. The measure of my strength as a man, ...and *yes*, "love," for you won't be measured by my jealousy or absence of it, but rather the fact that I own and endure it, allowing you to have the freedom you need and never placing it upon you in some encumbering, hindering way.

I don't think you are entirely immune from a bit of jealousy yourself with regard to me and other women, even if not physically, jealous of the possibility of me sharing some of the emotional connection that we do. I think that is the key to a successful relationship like we have discussed, that if you should ever find that person with whom you can be "significant" in each "other's" lives, that you reserve a portion of each other, the best portion, for only that one other person. To do otherwise, to spread everything you have so thin, to give it to everyone, takes what is rare and special and makes it commonplace. What is rare is of value because it is *rare*, and should be treated as such, what is common, what is available to everyone is of a much lesser value. I was saddened the other day, when you said that you were afraid to feel that

168

powerful love again, afraid of being hurt. There are no guarantees, but I hope someday you will find the courage to surrender yourself to it, and in the surrendering, in that moment of "losing" yourself you in actuality "find" yourself. It is what life is truly all about.

When I told you I love you I put my heart and love on the line, where they belong, and not tucked away inside of me. Don't ever shrink back from it please, it is meant as that "blanket" to wrap yourself in, and never to slow, or restrain you. To be fearful or cautious of it is to sacrifice the gift. You don't arrive at this place in life where I am right now all at once. It happens gradually, you rise and fall and get up again, paying attention to the mistakes you have made and trying not to repeat them. For whatever reason, beyond either of our understandings of it, I have taken some path, some loop that has brought me onto this road at the same time as you ....synchronicity if you will. I am a little older, and if you listen carefully, I will try to share some of my perspectives and experience with you, not as a mentor ...but a fellow traveler.

Once in a great while in one's life, you stand in a moment, in a place in time, and you recognize the beauty and potential of something while it is in front of you, and not regrettably some time much later when it has passed. That is how I feel about our friendship, and I will treat it with the respect, dignity and care that it deserves. I look forward to walking this crooked path with you, as long as you will let me, whether from near someday, or quite realistically, from afar as we do now. I apologize for getting off on such a tear, but then again....once I got started it just came pouring out of me... HELP, I've sprung a leak :)) I hope it was not too deep, and I hope you will always afford me the right to say what I feel, and not ask me to temper my words, as I hope you will never do either.

In either case I am still interested in seeing you, unless, the time should come when the thought of NOT having me in your life as a friend/lover produces a greater sense of relief, than of sadness ...and that will be your call. Otherwise, I'll see you when I can ...and you can buy lunch :) Hope you have had a great day. As always...

Love,

-Jake

The boy was inside the girl's head like he had popped her eye out and was mind-fucking her, and just busted a big nut of confusion. It had worked, he had touched that spot in her again with his words, fucking *Cyrano*-dude, one of the pieces of the puzzle he provided so to speak. Reminding her of what she loved *about* him, how he made her feel, and in a sense telling her what she wanted. And in the process he had cleared a second hurdle, one neither of them had prepared for that would include his ability to *play well with others* ...or at least give the *appearance* of it.

For a time at least, he was nestled closer, and tossing verbal pebbles at her window once again, prompting her to come out and play ...with *him*, ...and then came "that" call, Glen was out of town for the evening...

Her kids' playhouse provided fittingly appropriate cramped quarters for their constrained relationship, an incubator as it were. He would deposit his **seeds** of doubt with great enthusiasm as she bent uncomfortably over a child's picnic table, biting her knuckle to keep from making her usual *Ummm's,* and *Ohhh's.* As coarse and unsettling as it sounds, it's the truth, and the "*truth*" is seldom delicate or tasteful ...there's just no sugarcoating some things.

And when it was over he quickly stole away into the night, to his truck parked at the shopping center half a mile away, and she back to her house and the sleeping children, her cheeks as red as a cherub's. While the encounter was brief, after all, they're called *quickies,* it would have long lasting effects... And just like that it was done, the faux seeds of a nonexistent dilemma, of a realistic concern planted. And it would spread like emotional kudzu...

He waited an appropriate amount of time for the fictitious "incubation" period before he dropped the "news" and explained he had some "discomfort" and wondered if she had any as well, he would tell her he had been to the doctor to get checked for an STD, and they were treating him for *chlamydia*, the test inconclusive. He had been routinely careful and used protection with everyone but her, which was true, and she should get herself checked. He hoped it would scare her into limiting her activities at least for a while and it worked. She was initially frightened as to be expected, how could she avoid the <u>remote</u> *possibility* that her husband might want to have sex? It had the desired effect Jake sought, and would eliminate the competition for a while, ...not forever, but a while.

Her test naturally came back negative, but the doctor gave her some antibiotics <u>just</u> <u>in</u> <u>case</u> *"because chlamydia isn't easily diagnosed,"* and she would tell her husband if the occasion arose that she had a yeast infection and was advised to avoid any intercourse. He had accomplished what he sought which was to cast an unseemly and disparaging light on the competition, and though she wouldn't be having sex with him for a while either, he had added another thread to the ties that were secretly binding them.

In the process however, she became all too aware of his increasingly larger presence in her secret life. Cautiously aware of it, and it concerned her more than a little. He had knowledge that could upset things. She knew that he loved her, she *loved* that he did, but who would've thought that "love" might be a bad thing, and what had she potentially gotten herself into? Any notions that he was or would be manipulating her situation were unthinkable, she trusted him, and she *needed* to at this point. But she recognized it presented a threat of sorts if she angered him and would require a delicate balancing act to avoid it, not to mention …a degree of censorship in what she divulged in the future as well.

He had an advantage to be sure, secretly able to read her emails he now knew things she didn't know he did. While he might have created an impediment to her pursuing her plans, he hadn't eliminated her desire to explore them, and she was a resourceful gal. In the meantime he would begin to look into who some of these guys were, he was a part-time investigator after all, and beyond the curiosity he had a genuine desire to protect her. She in turn only had some wariness. It didn't make it right, but it made perfect sense to him. He wanted to be the man she called when she had the time, but he had gone from being the guy she was thinking of while having sex with her husband, to being the guy she was telling about having sex with another man.

His inadvertent *slap* of the tongue regarding Olivia had been a wake up call for her. As if in some illicit courtroom he had volunteered his commission of a "*Miss*-demeanor" and set a precedent for her subsequent "*Miss*-behavior." Having opened the door to that line of questioning, he would now have to endure *her* testimony regarding it. This was not part of the deal he thought. But he couldn't stay mad at her, even though he *felt* he had reason to, and before long it once again became that pursuit of the unattainable, challenging that competitive nature in the man. The hound in him had picked up that *scent* again, chasing her hot ass like she was a bitch in heat …and there were other dogs coming around.

He had become a spy in his very own *covert emotional espionage* drama, all the while living his life and fulfilling his role as father, businessman, friend ...and still her most trusted confidante, after all who could she tell her secrets to *other* than him?

But what a wicked web we weave, when first we practice to deceive ...and start fucking around with someone's head and *personal* life. He was aware of the hypocrisy and hazard of it all, but essentially helpless, in part now sleeping with other women **because** he couldn't get time with her, and not just because it was in his *nature*. She had begun to seek out other men **because** he was sleeping with other women and because he had sparked that curiosity inside her ...revealing something about *her* nature. She now had an ongoing fundamental need to prove to herself that she was <u>special</u>, *not* him ...*or* **them**, and the preacher's daughter was hell-bent on doing so. It was like a knot in the middle of an endless rope, it couldn't be untied, no clear beginning or end to it, intertwined and entangled in a *messy* way ...regardless of the time or distance between them. Things would end up twisted as a Franklin County back road ...and **no** <u>one</u> could see around the curve.

CHAPTER 8

LOVE REMOVAL MACHINE

They say that we are most attracted to people who see us as we see ourselves, who see us as we want to be seen, and she did that for him, and he undeniably did that for her. He of course recognized it, but they had abruptly gone from getting together every opportunity they could, to an early off-season of sorts, entering into a period of torpor in **their** sexual activities with **_each other_** ...that thing similar to hibernation, but not quite. He didn't like it one bit, but what were his options? Exit stage right and surrender? He was incapable of doing so, bound up by the ropes that had grown out of their "No Strings Attached" beginning.

The lunch dates and drinks after work that began to take place all centered around some upcoming availability she was going to have and she was letting him know about it. However, it didn't take long before he began to recognize that he wasn't hearing from her either by phone or email in the time leading up to the occasion discussed, and then it had passed, with some bullshit story attached. It began to ire him, but the role provided proximity to her and he wouldn't relinquish it, and if he became the source of that necessary flattery then he still had a value to her, and if he had a value to her …well he was a smart endearing guy, he'd figure something out.

In all fairness to Jake, at its onset she was as knee-deep in the shit as he was, they were both addicted to it, a crowd of two caught up in the *mob effect* the passion produced, only he wasn't fighting it and she was. Her life and all that was at risk, more so than his, served as the walls of a prison that restrained them. But she was on the inside, and he was on the outside, free to do what he pleased, aside from intentionally breaking her out, still trying desperately to rationalize irrational behavior, to be a conscionable unconscionable man. In all fairness to her, the man was changing, not irreparably or permanently, but like a virus she had infected him. He was expected to be accepting of her marital situation, and while she would come to express an interest in his activities, she would have to be accepting of the fact he was single and free to do as he pleased ...at least in theory. It would be an impediment to the natural emotional evolution of their relationship, *aside from her marriage*, and that freedom of his would become his enemy, his albatross, where she was concerned. Like a child who watches with envy as their friend gets invited to the *cool kids'* table at lunch and can't come along, she would begin to make new *friends* in an effort to prove she didn't need him as much anymore. And she abruptly concluded that Jake had become a little too important for her own good, but he had sparked something inside her, and there would be no going back.

He couldn't see her when he wanted, couldn't call when he wanted, the emails were the only avenue he had to her head and heart, and it would be an ongoing offensive against the invisible competition, against the concerns and suspicions he imagined she had *perhaps* developed towards him. Alarmingly aware of his increasingly unhealthy behavior, but like some sexual clairvoyant, he sensed the presence of other unseen and unacknowledged playmates.

He would have simply been paranoid were it not for the fact they actually existed. In some cosmic flip-flop, a cross-pollination of sorts occurred at this point in their affair, leaving each with remnants of the other, now she was going up and he was going down on that proverbial elevator. Just like a vaccine that introduces a small amount of a virus into the body to induce the body's defenses to attack it, he would have the self-defeating effect of satisfying her needs to the point she would grow immune to his specific contributions.

It was the first instance perhaps of him pimping himself out on her behalf, an instance where the deed itself afforded him no immediate benefit, but it was an investment. A step towards what he sought, and like a hog rooting around in the slop looking for something delectable he would have to eat the shit first. He had been the type of kid with tears in his eyes that wouldn't cry "uncle" to make it stop, and she would metaphorically damn near twist his arm off. But the kid had matured into a patient impatient man with an enormous tolerance for pain, and he would need it.

In nature, those who refuse, or are unable to adapt become extinct or useless, and while the notion didn't sit well with him it was either that or concede his place in the rotation of her developing "roster." So he would have to go into that "*I can't quit you babe, ...so I'm gonna have to put you down for a while*" mode, it was driving him crazy. And he needed to get laid. Their episodes had been characterized by very emotionally charged intense periods, and no matter what, he always walked away feeling like a stud horse kicking in his stall, and he derived a tangential benefit from them. Other women could sense a heightened level of confidence in the already quietly confident man. And it was time for him to cash in on those dividends with a gal or two he knew could conduct the transaction.

He had met Maureen and her roommate Lisette at the Crooked Creek Saloon, or the "Creek" as the locals called it. It was Raleigh's largest nightclub, a meat market and if you couldn't get lucky there …God help you. It was a club divided into theme sections, a country bar, a pool hall, a large contemporary dance section with DJ, and a smaller disco section. He had wandered through the place ...as usual, scoping it out, doing his math, until he settled in the disco section. It was an area of the club he didn't frequent often as he was more into the contemporary music than the retro-atmosphere of the disco section. But it was smaller, like a barrel of fish, and the women, surprisingly younger for the genre, on this evening outnumbered the men.

To be seen you had to join the game, and he asked a number of ladies to dance and was having a good time, when in between songs he was approached by an attractive long dark haired Hispanic woman, her name was Lisette, she told him that her friend Maureen wanted to dance with him, it seemed a bit odd, but perhaps Maureen was shy ...not to be the case it would prove. But as luck would have it Lisette was the one he was more attracted to, don't you hate it when that happens?

He would ask Lisette *"What about you, would you like to dance?"* *"I'm spoken for,"* she replied flashing a pawnshop engagement ring. He was in an ambiguous period in his life, and that was currently not an issue for him he thought to himself before he returned the words to her, *"That's okay, you're spoken for and I'm talked about, we'd make a great couple."* She laughed unguardedly, *"Thanks, but no thanks."* Her sassy New York Puerto Rican accent reminded him of the good-looking sister in **Ugly Betty**. Apparently she had accepted some soldier's proposal before he left for overseas, she hadn't seen him or any man in nine months, and she looked to be ripe. But Maureen was on the auction table, so **"M"** for Maureen it is he thought.

They were best friends from Brooklyn who had moved here a few years back, and worked as hairstylists at a salon that he didn't really care to hear the details of. But before the night got too late, they escorted our friend to a doublewide out in the country near Holly Springs, forty minutes from the club. They got extremely comfortable, no need to mask intentions, the ladies now in t-shirts and underwear, Jake reduced to nothing but his unbuttoned jeans.

The women enjoyed a joint together, and asked Jake if he wished to partake, he would have gladly accepted in another time, but had sworn off it since the divorce, and his efforts at being a role-model to his soon to be middle-schooler. *"I enjoy the altered states, but I prefer the southern ones,"* he smiled, again Lisette abbreviating her laugh as Maureen appeared perturbed about the apparent chemistry between the two. He couldn't help but notice Lisette had some big tits under her t-shirt, and she was squirming in her chair like a four year-old that needed to pee. She liked the sight of the man's physique, and was reconsidering her position on the matter, but Maureen was taking note of everything and dismissed her to her bedroom like a child or a pet. She was apparently the alpha bitch ...or she owned the trailer.

She and Jake had a couple of beers, relaxed a bit more, but it was now 2:00 a.m. and the man had been brought there for a purpose, and she was ready to put him to use. They would not retire to the privacy of the bedroom, probably because she wanted her girlfriend to hear what was going on as they crawled up on the couch. It was not the man's best performance, he was not all that motivated, questioning himself all the while as to why he wasn't coiled up with the other woman, but he needed to make a good enough showing to impress the audience as the door to Lisette's bedroom was now cracked and he could see her in the dim light flipping through a magazine, but studying him instead. It was one of those occasions where Jake shot over par, a respectable outing, making certain as he rose the *spectator* got a good look at him in all his glory, as Maureen dragged him off to her bedroom to tell him all about herself before falling asleep.

He lay there in the small uncomfortable bed for a time before he got up intending to escape the light of day. He quietly exited Maureen's room to find Lisette sitting in the den, no TV, no nothing, her finger posed in the corner of her mouth suggestively like some hooker in an Amsterdam brothel window, and like the Holly Springs tourist he was, he was going to have to pay her a visit. The forty-five year-old aroused at the sight of her, great refractory time he thought, impressed with himself.

She had small nipples for such huge breasts, the areola, the brown part, about the size of a quarter, and the nipple itself the size of a field pea, and they were incredibly sensitive, almost to the point she didn't like them touched, as if it tickled too much. Pulling a page from the reference section of the aforementioned library, he gently wet them down and began to nibble on them like a mouse to cheese, trying not to trip the trap.

She wiggled and writhed like his dog rolling around on her back in the yard scratching her "itch" as he gave her his inches, *and fed her well.* She would announce her warm, moist *arrival* with that same sassy accent in ...*broken* ...*incomplete* ...sentences, it was **sexy**, but Maureen's appearance at the door declaring it was time to leave prematurely ruined the moment for Jake, who had not yet *arrived.* It was 4:25 a.m., he thought it rude and unfair, but she was tossing his clothes at him now, and it was apparently time to go ...and he could take his *hard-on* with him. Lisette put her business card in his back pocket as he left noticeably disappointed, but he would know how to get up with her, and tonight presented such an occasion. He would see her ...absent Maureen, and they would enjoy each other's company for an evening of much needed distraction, and finish the game of "twister" they had begun. Laura, Linda, ...Lisette, "**L**" like a **L**ollipop had been good to the boy.

Aware that *out of sight* sometimes meant *out of mind*, and obsessed at the fact that others were barking up her tree as well, he continued to email Rae, in that *"I'm shaking the bush boss,"* way to let her know he was still out there and hankering to see her when possible. But she was busy developing outside interests ...like Tony. Jake had confirmed some desirability she thought existed about her, and Tony looked like he saw it as well. He was a massage-therapist at the Country Club she belonged to, and she enjoyed a good pampering after her tennis, golf, or workout. He was in his late twenties, and had a reputation among some of the wives for providing "additional services" *free of charge* on occasion. He was always flirting with Rae, as his hands glided all over her body, she didn't look like she had given birth to three children, and he told her so. He questioned why he never saw Mr. Johnston at the club, apparently his idea of physical activity was grading papers she replied. They had a natural physical chemistry, and he apparently understood discretion and she targeted him as a potential playmate. As she rolled from back to front, underneath the sheet, she asked him to rub out her thigh, tense from her workout, and she nearly left a wet spot when he touched it. This time when he would make a suggestive comment she would ask him if he was interested in getting a drink later, he could talk the talk, could he walk the walk.

Jake and Rae had met for a drink earlier in the week where she told him Glen would be a guest-speaker at a conference at the University of Tennessee in Knoxville that weekend, and if things went the way she hoped, she'd be available, wondered if he might be as well. But Jake was sensing a pattern developing, one in which she would halfheartedly feign an attempt at hiding the fact she had made other plans after he had properly nourished her ego. He told her he anticipated being free, as it was Rene's weekend, but in the interim he got the dreaded call he had anticipated regarding his mother. Ann was fading fast, her body shutting down, not because of disease or trauma, but the simple accumulation of a difficult life's mileage.

She had a curious look of anxiousness about her when he arrived, like a child's first visit to the doctor, an understandable concern about the unknown. And like he had been with his father, he was there when she too passed. The child comforting the parent in one of life's more ironic twists.

Both of his parents had now died in his arms, and he would not have traded anything for it. It was both a blessing and a curse. A blessing in a sense that he knew they were not alone, that he had gotten to say goodbye, but a curse in the sense that it was undeniably painful to see the people who loved you most in the world leave it, and you. He felt alone, and would need the comfort of someone who cared about him, and after the necessary couple of notifications to those concerned, Rae Anne was the **third** person he called.

He desperately wanted to see her when the weekend finally came, and he got the call all right. She said Glen would _not_ be going out of town. So he headed to Leon's, but it wasn't long before he had to satisfy that innate curiosity, and if curiosity killed the cat, it straight murdered the dawg. He would drive by her house and notice Glen had apparently purchased an antique muscle car, how unlike him. Or ...someone else had gotten the call that he had hoped to. He drove to the shopping center and parked, then walked that half-mile walk to her house, navigating the landscape and terrain he was now familiar with. He admired the car in the driveway as he passed it, and then continued to the backyard where in his mental imbalance he thought to see if he could catch a glimpse of what was going on. He got an eyeful he would not soon forget ...*if possibly ever.*

The lights were on in the den, the sheers drawn across the glass doors to the deck. And there they were, sitting on the couch watching TV like High School sweethearts. The guy seemed extremely interested in what was on TV ...and she *didn't*. This was her discretionary time, and she had other ideas in mind. She slid behind him and began massaging his shoulders, signaling her readiness and intentions. This was a service call, "Service is requested, assistance required aisle 5. *I didn't invite you here because you don't have cable,*" or something along those lines Jake thought to himself.

She removed her shirt, those beautiful breasts he was all too familiar with unleashed and lain on the man's shoulders, yet the fella hardly seemed to notice ...*at first*. She whispered something to him, turned the TV off, and the sexual *wet work* began.

As he watched, "casual sex" suddenly seemed like a peculiar combination of words, like "ice warm beer," the words made unnatural neighbors. It's the most intimate thing two humans can do, hardly *casual*, and yet we do it with the ease of animals, much as we in fact are, and Jake was far from an opponent of the practice... having made an art form and part-time career of it, building his **a**typical life around it. But if men are turnkey operations with the sexual act, he was finding himself to be as confounding as a **Rubik's Cube** when it came to the *emotions* associated with ***this*** variation. Beyond that age of innocence and first loves, no man has any illusion that they are the first to have been with a woman, but most have some natural aversion to the idea of some other fella falling up in there after them if they have some feelings for the gal, and as unaccustomed as he was to the sensation ...he *felt* it.

A woman has to allow a man inside her, and when that *invitation* is extended to someone else, it *can* eat at a lover's psyche, confidence, and his *stability*, like a crippling blow to his emotional weak spot. Make no mistake, with rare exception, women are the givers, and men the recipients of sex, and it's one thing to know there has been another *recipient* …and quite another to <u>actually</u> be a witness to it, and as he watched another man get the "gift" that he felt should have been his, he was temporarily paralyzed by the unfamiliar commotion it produced of jealousy, anger …and *disbelief.* It was surreal.

Like one of those horror stories where the patient regains consciousness on the operating table but can't move or tell anyone …Jake was having open-heart surgery, and she was **not** a surgeon… but a coroner instead, …a *love removal machine* in effect. He stood there in the darkness, not knowing whether to cry or touch himself at the sight of it all, like the singular audience to a live sex show, he couldn't look away. Forget the unimportance of an historic timeline, but he imagined what it would have been like for Caesar to be stabbed to death

while made to watch Marc Antony fuck Cleopatra...
Et tu Rae? And then he caught a glimpse of his
own reflection in the glass backdoor ...the image
disturbingly unrecognizable, as if a stranger to
himself.

When his feet finally began to move they carried
him around to the driveway. The guy had a
beautiful automobile, a midnight blue Pontiac GTO,
dressed out, but the doors were unlocked, so he
glanced inside the glove box for the registration.
His name was Anthony Marcus Donelli ...not *quite*
Marc Antony, but too damn close for coincidence it
seemed, as though a senate comprised of Destiny,
Fate, and some guy named Anthony Marcus/Tony,
were inadvertently killing *him* by "*stabbing*" Rae.
All he could think was first things first, he was
gonna have to *Tonya Harding*-style kneecap this
bullshit, the unfamiliar sensation of it all producing
a troubling and uncharacteristic reaction in the man,
foreign and unlike him ...*prior* to meeting her that
is.

He walked back to the shopping center that housed a neighborhood pool hall among the other shops, etc., where he and Rae sometimes met. He would spend the next few hours there contemplating his next move until returning, armed with a juvenile plan in mind. In that period of time he had bounced around occupations as a younger man, he had worked for a time as an independent contractor for a satellite TV installer, he knew that there was a test-jack in the phone box on the side of the house, it was the first thing he had checked every time he got a service call about a customer unable to download pay-per-view, to make certain there wasn't a problem with the phone line which lead to the satellite box.

He went to the 24-hour Drug Store that anchored the shopping center and purchased a $10 touch-tone phone with a cord, went back to the pool hall and waited until it was closing time, then made the walk back to her house. He had remembered her story about the older couple calling the police the night of her tantrum, and he knew the police would keep record of the call. He was aware it was extremely unhealthy behavior for a forty-five year-old man

…like **T**emporary **R**estraining **O**rder unhealthy, but so was her behavior he told himself. He found the plastic phone box on the outside wall of the neighbor's house, and using a dime, loosened the screw that held it shut. He had assembled the phone in necessary fashion, no cradle, no electric cord, just the wire that would connect to the phone and the jack. He had brought a pen to put under his tongue to disguise his voice when he spoke as he knew the call would be recorded, and dialed 911.

He told the call-taker that he thought there might be a disturbance at his neighbors' house, had heard moans and what sounded like muffled cries for help, and he knew the husband to be gone. Gave them the address, and hung up. He knew the old couple's phone number would show up on the PD's caller ID, and provide the necessary credibility. He then disconnected the phone, secured the box and left for the woods to wait for the police to arrive.

Jake would not soon forget the expression on their faces when two police cars descended upon the residence, Tony hoping to get away unseen, and Rae Anne standing there with the infamous just-had-sex/bed-head hair in her short white robe, stunned and frightened about what to do next, as he sat hidden from sight like some thirteen year-old vandal who has strewn toilet paper all over someone's trees, impishly admiring his handiwork. It was now 2:45 a.m. on a Saturday night/Sunday morning and people had begun to stir, it would not go unnoticed. But before it all played out, Jake had headed back to his truck, and home, with an undeniable satisfaction about himself. It wasn't pretty, he wasn't proud of it, it wasn't who he was, or at least not who he use to be, but she had damn sure affected who he was.

He had read her emails, knew of her intentions, had **seen** the competition, and began to think in terms of how he would need to adapt and create perceived deficiencies in their game and her efforts to play with them. The dose of imaginary Chlamydia had merely proven to be a speed-bump, and not the roadblock he had hoped. A course of antibiotics and a condom had bypassed the issue, and he'd shot his *passive aggressive* wad with the attempt. Like some perverse emotional warfare, or PSYOP, he was now a romantic terrorist attempting to produce

196

an affliction only he had the antidote for ...*anxiety*, and thereby reinforce remedies only he could provide such as familiarity, comfort ...and *safety*.

He would write her an email later that day, they were initially supposed to get together that evening after all, inquiring about how her weekend with the hubby had gone, now in full knowledge of the bullshit story she had fed him about Glen not leaving town. He never let on that he was any the wiser, his behavior sinister, creepy, and a threat to all she held dear, and in that same psychotic vein he told himself she had it coming. She'd think twice about it next time, or so he hoped...

Rae would call in a day or two, perhaps because she wanted to check the tone of his voice, who knows, but he took a perverse pleasure in listening to her squirm over the phone as she continued her lie about the weekend's "mundane" activities, and he informed her of his comfortable but uneventful weekend, and that he missed having the opportunity to see her... She would never discuss the actual events of the evening with him, he would never know how it had entirely played out, but he had accomplished what he sought. I don't doubt for a moment he didn't cross her mind in the aftermath though. She wasn't stupid.

It was now mid-February, only ten weeks since that first weekend, but like one of those rides at the **State Fair** it had an extreme amount of twists and turns, highs and lows, for its short duration. Once she began to step outside of their relationship, he was removed from the starting line-up and became an involuntary mascot of sorts, no longer the star player. He now represented the magic mirror, you know, the "mirror, mirror, on the wall ...who's the fairest of them all?" variety. He had unwittingly become her cheerleader, helping her properly inflate her ego in his own attempts to get back in her good graces, the kids' playhouse, or on her floor as it often seemed, and in the process helping her ramp up for her next "event" absent him. And "no," he had not forgotten she was married, but he *thought* himself more than just the occasional guest, as if he'd earned a special distinction and place in her life, and should thus be afforded the accompanying perks and preferential treatment of a *preferred customer* ...or "frequent fucker" as it were.

If she'd had the wherewithal in the moment she would have noticed the signs, and maybe she did, but the long-term forecast appeared favorable and she proceeded anyway. While it might have begun as a respite from the drought in her life, a welcomed brief or occasional shower of much needed attention, the emotional meteorologist in her should have noticed the elements and the hazards presented by the gathering of circumstantial clouds and coincidental fronts, and the fact that Jake was the *only* variable common to each. That component, however indistinct and far removed from the actual *storm* itself, which still had a degree of *relative* proximity and consistency with it …like thunder, …never far behind the lightning.

All aspects that would eventually get out of hand with the fury, confusion, and potential for harm of a category 5 emotional hurricane, the fact that she didn't revealed her level of connectedness as well… Liken it to standing with your nose on a billboard, you can't begin to see it clearly and make sense of it until you get some distance from it, the "**me to**" you first saw and couldn't make sense of, becomes "Welco**me to** Hell."

CHAPTER 9

POCKETFUL OF SALT

Earl had been the precursor to Chunk in Jake's life. They had grown up together, literally grown up together, some of the first memories each of them had included each other, and those are typically from the age of two or three. He had known Jake before he went through that difficult period as a child, and remained his only friend through it. They were extremely similar, "brothers of different mothers" they would say. Jake would say he wasn't afraid of any man, only God and the government, but if there was a man that concerned him it was Earl. They had once held each other in headlocks for nearly 30 minutes before Earl's mom had called him home for supper, neither submitting.

While Jake was *failing* his first attempt at college, Earl had gone to work at a textile mill in Greensboro, but they were both young, dumb and full of cum, and neither could concentrate on one thing for very long. In that period between the time he had broken up with his girlfriend, and before he moved to Raleigh, Jake and Earl thought to give the military a try, the economy was bad, it was peacetime and the Air Force and Naval recruiters advertised a buddy-system, sign up with your buddy and stay together through basic training and your first duty assignment. They started at the Air Force recruiter's office, took the ASVAB, Armed Services Vocational Aptitude Battery, and each did well, but Jake's criminal record for some youthful mischief would keep him from getting in, next stop the Navy Recruiting station, same story...

It seemed the military had a surplus of enlistees at the time and could afford to be selective, and while Earl was accepted into both branches they were determined to proceed together, but everyone was now pointing them in the direction of the Marines, and Jake was growing less interested at that thought, planes and boats were cool, and he was thinking in terms of how girls swarmed over the flyboys and sailors. But he had known a friend who had joined the Marines three years earlier. They had thrown him a party when he came home from boot camp, and the nineteen year-old spent the entire night in a tree, Jake would bring him the occasional beer, but the kid spent the entire night in a tree ...at his own party, as if on recon or some shit, until when no one was looking he disappeared, perhaps thinking he didn't fit in anymore. They didn't see him again until he had completed his two-year tour of duty ...he had come out of it very different than he went in. When they say you can take the man out of the Marines, but you can't take the Marine out of the man they weren't kidding, and Jake was looking for a change of scenery, but not a change in his psychological makeup. He wasn't one to be told what to do anyway, and he drew the line at that point where if he couldn't go where he wanted, he wouldn't go at all, and before too long he headed to Raleigh to live and look for work.

Earl on the other hand, was intrigued by it. He had wanted to start with the Marines, **"The Few, The Proud, The Marines,"** like a romantic siren's song to him. His father had served in the Corps before becoming a State Trooper, and it almost seemed his calling. Their buddy plan had dissolved and Earl headed off to Parris Island S.C. for training. He would travel around the world, Okinawa, return to Parris Island for Drill Instructor School and serve a tour of duty in that regard before the first Gulf War broke out, afterwards stationed at Lejeune for a time, going wherever they sent him, until returning to the "sandbox" post 9/11. They would lose touch for long periods of time, but every once in a while he would hear from the man. Earl had told Jake on one occasion about a routine he had developed along the way. Every time he went into a bar, wherever it was, first thing he would do was order a shot of tequila, salt, and the lime, take a pinch of salt and throw it over his left shoulder for good luck, and then unnoticed pour some in his hand, and put it in his pocket. It sounded like some superstitious Sailor/Marine thing to Jake at the time you know, but Earl explained that he did so because he often found himself in those establishments that got rowdy, the salt served as a potential diversion it seems, in those fracases that would break out in the abundance of restlessness that accompanied shore leave when abroad, before a deployment, or upon a return, and that DI in him was always in control.

Jake called him on the bullshit, they had grown up in a time when professional wrestling was big, and he remembered Mr. Fuji, the consummate villain who had made a trademark of throwing salt in his opponents' eyes. More importantly he knew Earl didn't need the help. He had readily disabled scores of larger men, but he could sympathize that at their age he wasn't interested in fairness, he was interested in prevailing. He had taught young men and women how to kill, and defend themselves from those who wanted to kill them. For him fairness had been reduced to a very brief statement that he was about to do you harm. He was no longer interested in proving himself to the younger men, only settling the matter. He seemed to have grown weary of fighting unnecessary battles and as a sort of flashback to their adolescence, he gave Jake an involuntary reminder, presented the salt with a magician's flick of the wrist, slapped him twice before Jake could figure out what was happening, point well taken ...and it was a routine Jake incorporated into his preparation before going out, largely as a tribute to his friend who had survived Fallujah, but not the motorcycle crash that killed him after his 20 years of service. He had been a pallbearer at Jake's father's funeral. At his family's request, Jake had served as a pallbearer at his. He must've been a helluva guy, because one helluva guy thought him so.

Now there's been some discussion about a man's physicality, of intimidation, of the way men interact and perceive one another, and the way women respond to it. Admittedly it seems a bit antiquated and barbaric, we are in the 21st century after all, well beyond the gladiator and warrior-prince periods, but make no mistake, we are at best civilized beasts, but beasts nonetheless. We pay to watch men beat the hell out of each other, our favorite sports are the violent ones, one man imposing his will on the other, taking something of his in the process. And the female of the species for the most part, despite strong protest to the contrary, has not outgrown that instinctive draw towards the male who can provide and protect either, only that as we have "evolved," that definition has broadened beyond the physical threats to include any man who can offer financial and emotional stability, and thus shelter from harm.

While we seem to deny and renounce its existence, we simultaneously celebrate it as a culture. And Jake hypothesized that it boiled down to four basic categories, and men routinely fall into one or more, the *strong*, the *quick*, the *smart* and the *prey*, if you have some doubt to its existence, an examination of inner-city gangs or our prison system affords an unadulterated glimpse at its ugliness, an unintentional social experiment, like ants in a classroom glass ant-farm, beneath the surface, it is on display. We may attribute it to their particular circumstances, but the circumstances only exaggerate the underlying inclinations as opposed to creating them.

In the subplot of this "dawg eat dog" world, the man who has never suffered defeat has an aura about him, a reputation, a **myth**, and a distinction that in and of itself can assuage many confrontations, and becomes a second entity that any opponent seems to battle with as well. A presence that enters the imaginary ring ahead of the man, and often strikes the first unseen blow, but to the man himself it can also be a heavy burden that hangs around his neck like an obligation of expectations to be met, an Achilles heel, that in the event his persona is not enough to demand surrender or respect, can weaken him, as he also battles that unblemished record at the heart of it all as much as any opponent.

The first loss, and every such man will have one unless he refuses to participate or retires prematurely from the game, is debilitating. It fractures the almighty yet fragile ego, the psyche filled with confidence that had grown to be a source of strength now clouds with doubt, the psychological beating of greater consequence than the physical. But contradictory as it may seem, in a minority of men, such losses can ironically prove to be a powerful and liberating thing, because the fear of losing has now been displaced with the knowledge that they can and will get up. And that *education*, that resulting loss of fear or *fearlessness* can be a dangerous thing …especially when confined to a man of size and strength.

As is sometimes the case, boys who lose their fathers young grow up with an under-developed sense of what it takes to be a man, often overcompensating, and hardheaded and stubborn, Jake was not an easy study in that regard and it was a lesson he learned at a painful price. He had not learned the natural and ordinary boundaries of when to fight and when to walk away, had never learned to run from trouble and consequently often found himself mired in it. Young and full of *piss and vinegar,* he was brash and cock-strong and the combination resulted in a lot of unnecessary confrontations, and the few and subsequent losses he had suffered were severe and brutal, but they were also losses that had come out of situations where he was not only in some weakened state, but truly incapable of defending himself. And others who were looking to make a name for themselves, for a notch on their reputation, took advantage of the opportunities. He had the good fortune to learn from his mistakes, a smart man does, and as he matured he would most certainly make more mistakes, but lessen the opportunity to repeat the same ones.

He wasn't a troublemaker or asshole, but just an extremely complex contradiction, veiled by his apparent simplicity. Make no mistake about it. He was a nice guy, loving father, wonderfully loyal and compassionate human, a lighthearted man, and extremely bright, he had been a number of men's best friend along the way, and a few women's. Unassuming and unpretentious, very likely to be laughing with his pals and picking fun at himself, but as he had learned at an early age, the most "dangerous" men in any room never have to tell anyone, they don't have to behave the part, like the appearance of a stray and mangled dog wandering into a yard, others know that win or lose, he will put up a fight and its best to leave him alone. He made no assumptions as to whether or not he was such a man, to do so is to wear an invitation for trouble on your forehead, but suffice it to say he knew how to recognize them, and if there's any truth to the saying that "it takes one to know one," for reasons unspoken, he was always left alone.

Being an exception to rules, he would acknowledge them, and that during the course of his life he had been strong, been quick, been prey, and become smart, they are not fixed states, nor mutually exclusive, but often transient phases in which sometimes the "strong" the "quick" and the "smart" become the **prey** because of the threat they present. They exist in all aspects of society, from the boardroom to the bedroom, the playground to the battleground, while seldom rising to the surface or being fully activated, the instincts are undeniable, and pervasive. And emotions are almost always its trigger, the pin pulled from the grenade.

In that collection of phrases he kept, he had read the poem *"If"* by *Rudyard Kipling* as a young man, it seemed like a companionate pamphlet to the instructions his dad had left him with, and two of the lines stood out, ***"If you can keep your head when all about you are losing theirs, and blaming it on you"*** and ***"yet don't look too good, nor talk too wise ...you'll be a man my son!"***   It spoke to the experience that had been visited upon him, and he had thus learned it was in his best interest to remain unnoticed as much as possible.

But this business with her, the awareness of these other men and his increasing obsession of them together were quickly becoming his enemies. The knowledge of what she was doing was bad enough, his imagination of it <u>worse</u>, and his OCD became an emotional autism in a sense, like "Raen-man." The emotion and the increased *static* it created were shaking that pin loose, and he was beginning to think taking a metaphorical piss in this girl's yard wasn't going to be enough to keep the other dogs out, he might have to take a shit ...and bring a *pocketful of salt* just in case.

His life had become that scratched DVD that catches and keeps replaying the same scene of the movie over and over, *Tony and Rae*, and for the life of him, he couldn't fast forward beyond it or skip to the next scene. It had to be painful. All those aspects of his personality that had worked against him in the past had corrupted those that had, and it went from light to dark, from yang to yin.

They'd had their usual pep-rally regarding her upcoming "me" time, but when she cancelled at the last moment *"because one of the children was sick,"* ...in a contrasting pattern of his own that was developing, he **had** to see for himself. The absence of cars in the driveway was sufficient enough for him to continue his "investigation." Jake knew her schedule and routine, for a smart gal she was remarkably predictable, though it was more a product of the fact she had a small comfort-zone, and a big desire to control her situations that made her so, and not naiveté.   He found her at a neighborhood bar they had occasionally rendezvoused. *Neighborhood* in the sense it was a neighborhood establishment …just not her neighborhood where she might run into her actual neighbors or fellow PTA members. Anxious, in a voyeur meets peeping Tom moment where he was about to step out of the anonymity and darkness of what had been her backyard and make himself an unscripted character in her play. He strolled in and found what he had feared …but suspected. She was there, and not alone. Squirreled away in the corner with the same fella he'd seen at her house, earring, tribal tattoo on his right bicep, and short black hair like one of those **Paul Mitchell** salon photos at the place Jake got his hair cut.

Up close he had an ethnic appearance about him, though watered down like second or third generation.   He was a good-looking guy, they looked good together, and he understood the attraction ...and hated it. There were only certain things he could compete with, and it riled him that she had chosen to break off their plans to spend them with this guy ...**again**, believing he had successfully cut him from the herd with his stunt. In an attempt to avoid looking pathetic, he called Ivey to see if she was available and willing to play the role of a paramour. She had extended the offer in a sense with her text, and only lived ten minutes away and was happy to oblige for a little while before heading out to meet up with her friends.

He could feel the *static* blurring into a panic as he waited, like some commercial strength tool it was inappropriate for everyday "household" use but it had its utility in his life. Probably the remnant of some primitive or ancestral ingredient of being a man that made Ivan *"**terrible**,"* or ...Alexander *"**great**."* One man's curse is another man's blessing, for Jacob it was a bit of both, the most god-awful sensation and the first thing he would have changed about himself, and the last thing he would have wanted to ...the chink that if ironed out would've weakened the armor of the man, but it was his and it was not an unfamiliar sensation so he calmed himself before he had the appearance of the bad-ass at the end of the bar about to have a panic-attack.

Rae hadn't noticed him yet, and he hoped she wouldn't until Ivey arrived. The young man made his way to the bar to order another round of drinks, as Jake literally bullied his way to the counter to take a spot next to him and ordered a beer. Uninvited, he leaned over and whispered to the guy *"If you nibble on that woman's earlobe when she arches her back, then whisper 'you fuck like a porn star,' she'll coo like a songbird for you."* "Who the fuck are you?" Tony replied, now revealing a hint of an accent like some character on **Jersey Shore**. *"I'm the man she'll call when you don't get the job done,"* Jake responded with a deliberately sarcastic snarl and a wink, sensing the young man represented an exception to her *"intelligent conversation"* criteria, and that he might have to spell it out for him ...or say it again slower.

The man squared his shoulders as if he might start something, ...expecting the older man to flinch, then relaxed as Jake stood there smiling, his thumb hanging on his left pocket in case he needed to channel some Earl. At forty-five he had a good fight or two left in him, hopefully the situation wouldn't merit the expenditure of that rain-check voucher on this occasion. *"Give it a try buddy, one soldier of love to another,"* Jake continued, subtly egging him on. The man looked at him like he was sick in the head, took their drinks back to the table, and sat surprisingly silent, occasionally glancing up at Jake as if pondering the advice and its origin. It was the worst advice he'd ever given another man, he almost felt guilty ...<u>almost</u>.

He hoped the boy would try it, it would most assuredly not please the woman, he knew it was a tender kiss on the neck below the ear, a hand underneath the small of her back to gently angle her, a short thrust, while he whispered something sweet to her with a simultaneous hit bottom plunge, and boom, just like a simple erotic equation, A+B=Big "O", she'd tense, breathless, then relax with a long slow sigh, call God's name or his, and drop that egg, her legs falling open like an oyster offering up it's pearl.

She'd noticed him by now, and it had caused a bit of a distraction as if she had a trace of *static* about her as well. He winked and then sent her a text, it read: *"I hope you think of me right before you don't cum ...and right after you wish you had."* Then he stood there at the end of the bar, a look of satisfaction about him like a man who had just robbed a bank and made a clean getaway before anyone knew of the theft, the pair none the wiser they had been relieved of their chance to fully enjoy the evening. Call it *social engineering* ...or a Trojan horse if you prefer, but behind the suggestion of helpfulness in his unsolicited guidance and the sarcasm in his text, was indeed malice ...even if it never made it any further than a second thought, the damage was already done. He had succeeded in making certain he was gonna be on both their minds tonight, and he laughed to himself at the accomplishment.

That was why she'd call him somewhere down the road, regardless of her anger and disdain for his intrusion on her evening, or the discomfort she felt, not about having lied to him, but his knowledge of the fact. Because when it was all said and done she had friends, she had a husband. What she was in need and desirous of was a lover. To feel appreciated and yet tenderly ravished in the process, and Jake had paid attention, been a good student of her, a consistent provider if you will, and she would come to resent him in a sense for his consistency, as if he had created a log-in to her g-spot which only he had the password for.

And right on cue, Ivey arrived, looking very much the part, and the visual aid she presented would fuck up Rae's evening even more, in an "I'll see your *young stud massage-therapist* and raise you a *babysitter/cheerleader/stripper*," kinda way, even her date had taken notice of the young woman. And with a wink and a nod he finished his beer and left for the apparent promise of hijinks, even though they would say goodbye in the parking lot, his mission accomplished. The evening had exposed her untruth and it pissed her off. She couldn't readily accept her obvious inability to lie to him. He had also deliberately rubbed his freedom in her face, and very attractively so. It was a contrived and orchestrated performance and nothing would happen that night, but now Rae had a visual to go with the reminder that he was out there living his life, while she remained like a restless animal trapped in a cage, only getting morsels and never a meal, but his victory would be largely symbolic. He had hoped they were beyond this as friends, the lying, pretense and charade, but it was apparent they weren't ...*beyond* it that is, not that they weren't friends.

Ivey had come through for him, and he would be grateful. It was unclear as to whether he saw her again after that. He was honest, but he was also very private. It would be a while before he saw Rae again though, and a while longer before she saw him, that distinction *now* needs to be made. He "poked" her every so often with an email of his **twelve-inch** variety, just to remind her he was still out there, but she couldn't forget even if she'd tried. She wouldn't know it, but he was secretly minding her business, looking after her, and going forward, she might have even thanked him if she had.

There's no denying the woman had it goin' on though, unknown to anyone but Jake ...even the 'Nental bunch was unsuspecting. Once he got beyond the initial pain and appall of it, the man was impressed on an objective level, he knew single women who weren't putting up those kinds of numbers, she wasn't bowling them all down at once, but she only needed a 7-10 split for a spare. Most men couldn't have handled it, but he saw her as a work of art. What was of primary importance for him was that he had the pleasure of enjoying it, however infrequently, and not that anyone knew or understood. He had decided for himself that a little bit of Rae in his life was better than none. In a fucked up way it was chivalrous, and his loyalty admirable, he was nobody's bitch or punk, but he was definitely one of a kind.

Let's face it, we all want to be picked for the team at recess to play kickball ...even if we don't like kickball. The desire to be liked and accepted is instinctual and necessary to our survival, the herd weeds out the weak and the unpopular and she had chosen someone else that evening. But there *are* individuals that exist irrespective of the proverbial damn labeling he despised, and he was such a man. Not oblivious or immune to it, but mindful of the fact that if you give someone too much influence in your life, if you care too much about what others think, you give them control over you... And just like that hard-earned confidence he had come about, that which is given can be taken away, that which is earned cannot. He had cast aside those shackles of social mores and norms and relied only upon himself and his internal compass, though the magnetic north might have been growing off.

Whether you side with **National Geographic** ...or **Cosmopolitan...** on the whole *alpha*, *beta*, *omega* male debate, there are undeniably those men who are equal to the alpha male in terms of strength, cunningness, and attraction. In any other life he would have grown to be an alpha, it was in his blood, his lineage, but life and circumstances had made of him a different man, in some ways a stronger man, the ostracized child who had come not to need the approval of others. In an animal kingdom sense they are perhaps the most feared male in nature, and yet considered the lowest members of the social order because they serve no purpose to the group, the family, pack or pride, but stand outside it as a distraction and a threat.

The could-be leader who doesn't want to be, whose existence presents a danger to the alpha that is. He was a singular creature, and like the *rogue* he was, he enjoyed the company of others, he just didn't require it, and she seemed like the perfect companion female, trapped in a family unit against her nature, wanting to run away, but incapable. The responsibilities and commitment to her children and their well-being, and Glen as the source of that, the bars to her beautiful suburban cage.

It made for an interesting entanglement. What had begun as an intense brief affair, *a love triangle* at its onset, had evolved into a sexual octagon or some shit. Her husband was oblivious. She thought she and her three faces of **Eve** or **Sybil**, or **United States of Tara**, had everyone fooled, and Jake stood there as the only individual accidentally aware of it, and not aware of it all. He loved her in spite of what he knew, and that's what makes this story unique. Perhaps he had just become un-well, but for the time being she was getting what she wanted from him *as he saw it*, she just wasn't giving it back ...and that would become an issue as time went on.

CHAPTER 10

PSYCHOLOGICAL WEEDING

As you can imagine, there was an uncomfortable period of silence following the occasion at the bar, and sometimes there is much to be said by the absence of communication. On her behalf, the woman who never said anything she didn't mean had told a lie to the one man she wanted to be honest with, perhaps not always truthful and forthcoming, but honest. Who also happened to be the one person who could cause more harm to her house of cards than anyone, and more importantly, she'd gotten caught telling it.

Not a big deal really, but yet it had undeniably left her feeling vulnerable and exposed. But that wasn't all. She was also experiencing some unexpected discomfort about seeing Jake in his natural element. It was one thing to tell him to live his life and know that he was, and another to see him living it. Not just that he was living it, but a vivid reminder that she wasn't. She wanted to maintain the notion that she was special in his life, it had empowered her, and she wasn't ready to relinquish the idea that part of the man belonged to her …and in reality she <u>was</u>, and he <u>did</u>. But that insecurity in the suburban wife/mother of three's mind was unexpected and it affected her, and that *affected* her. The fact that the *coincidence* of it all didn't seem entirely coincidental had left her unnerved as you might expect. And when she hadn't heard from him, the emotional mathematics of it didn't add up, which exacerbated all of the above. It produced a Xanax moment for the gal, or a Xanax couple of days as it were.

He on the other hand was letting it play out and enjoying the discomfort he had wrought, knowing that if he had been the one to contact her right away it would have been received with the same curt cautionary remark about getting too involved. Think of it like this, there's that moment when the parent is angry when the child if ten minutes late for their curfew, but after thirty minutes, that anger becomes concern, when the child finally walks through the door an hour late …concern becomes relief, the anger not gone, but no longer at the forefront. Right now she was concerned, and the longer she went without hearing from him the more she felt an unfamiliar culpability, as their unspoken "honor among thieves" code had been broken, and uncertainty about what he was thinking. Reverse Psychology 101. And she needed to speak with him, Glen's father had fallen ill. There was a potential storm on the horizon of her life, and only Jake would understand.

When he finally heard from her she did what a lot of people in a similar situation would do, she followed the lie with another lie... And he said nothing other than he was glad to hear from her. Sometimes manure is fertilizer, and sometimes it's just bullshit, and Jake knew the difference here to be insignificant. The boy who had never learned when to run from confrontation, had become a man who had learned how to step back and duck... The last thing the referee says to the fighters... "Protect yourselves at all times," or protect your interests as the case may be. Sometimes you concede a pawn to take something of greater value later. And what was of greater value to him at this point, his interest so to speak was mainly reminding her that *he* was the stud horse in her stable, and he needed to be taken out for a run and stretch his legs ...and hers.

The text he had sent was mean and distasteful, the *sexual* equivalent of an "I told you so," only in advance. After Tony's ten minute "fuss and grunt," and mumbling some business about her being a porn star while he slobbered on her neck, he scurried out to watch a UFC pay-per-view with his buddies. In the loneliness of the remainder of the wasted evening that followed she couldn't help but think of Jake. She just couldn't tell him so.

But he had anticipated that, or created it to be more precise, and when the time felt right he seized the opportunity to poke her with his metaphoric rod figuratively, so that he could perhaps *stick* her with his actual rod more literally. You'll remember he had ulterior motives in most everything he wrote at this point, so be mindful of the contradictions that seem obvious ...they were not so apparent to her.

Rae,

It was great seeing you, you looked *inviting* ...wish I had gotten the invitation ;) Nice-looking fella, hoped you enjoyed your evening. It was the first time I've seen you when we weren't together. Strangely difficult and distracting for me to say the least. Did you feel it, that sexual chemistry and tension between us? Remember, honesty is not a luxury or convenience with me. I "desire"... no... "*Need*" one relationship in my adult life without the bullshit and pretense ...even if it hurts. Of course you know I did, like a *Tesla ball* I could see it from across the room. And yet we've been reduced to penpals and phone calls of late, what's that all about? Grown tired of me? Was it something I didn't say? :))

You asked me to save a small place in my life for you, and I have. Like any path that's not traveled that often the weeds have grown over it but it's still there nonetheless.

I'd love to take a stroll with you if you get my drift... I stood across the room and watched you flitter and float like the butterfly you are ...hoping you would land on me, and still do.

Wanna get together? My account needs servicing ...is this customer service? ;) Can I schedule an appointment for "maintenance"? ;) Where else are you gonna find a guy who accepts you for who you are, accommodates your schedule and boundaries, yadda yadda yadda blah blah blah,... AND ...can write you letters that make you laugh and tear up at the same time... :)) ...my one distinctive...and for some, most redeeming quality ;)

Lovers come and go, but "love" is hard to find Rae. We're obviously gonna get separated on this "path" at times, just don't lose sight of me entirely ...unless you want to ;)) I'd like to stay tethered to you for the duration of this journey. I told you that I would never be the most successful, or

attractive man you would meet but for a few women whom I let get close to me, I am a curious mix of things they find most *attractive* ...are you one of them? Until you decide, I'll still allow myself to think about you, and the much-anticipated warm embrace of a familiar stranger ...among other things ;)

Love,

-Jake

It was now April, springtime in North Carolina, the Dogwoods were abloom and the Encore Azaleas were making their debut, presenting themselves like buxom beauties strutting their stuff at an Easter parade. While autumn was his favorite season, spring was undoubtedly his second, the revitalization and renewed sense of life it brought with it would breathe fresh air into their relationship. She needed some attention, cultivation from an experienced and familiar gardener. Easter was coming up and the holiday presented the opportunity to get together, and this time, much to his delight, he would get the job and not simply the call for an *estimate*. He had some long awaited business to take care of where she was concerned, some clearing of briers from his mind and *psychological weeding* so to speak.

From his perspective, he had needed her that February weekend. That opportunity should have been reserved for him considering the circumstance he thought. He had been there whenever she needed him and it was an occasion that merited a withdrawal from the friendship bank. If they were truly friends, she would've been there for him, the fact that she wasn't, and not just **wasn't** ...but sprawled out with another fella stung. He had buried one of the few remaining people that loved him just days before and was desperately in need of some affection, a lover's touch. But she wasn't interested in being brought down by his sentimentality and in all actuality neither was he. He needed some release of the tension he bore, and she needed a good fuck ...and she got an average one, or so it appeared to Jake.

He greeted her with a warm loving hug when she arrived, a cool calm exterior, and the offer of a cold beer masking his fevered mind. It had now been two months since it had happened, but his memory still burned with the image. He'd felt challenged, as if the younger guy brought something to the table he didn't, aside from the age difference, and as a consequence he set out to remove any doubts she might have of his ability to accommodate any and all of her needs. And so, …as he had scripted in his mind, while Nine Inch Nails "**Closer**" echoed in the background like the *caller* at an industrial rock square dance, instead of a "swing your partner, dosey doe," it would be crass to say he correspondingly *fucked her like an animal* as the lyrics suggested, but suffice it to say the event was "raw" in nature …punitive …and impolite. It must've sounded like a kitchen screen door banging in a windstorm for the duration of the CD.

And yet …the angst was born out of love and the same unquenchable desire for the woman, and though he would have ceased at any moment if she had asked, instead she took it like a champ. She was an intuitive woman, she knew that as strong as he was, as *different* as he was, he was silently struggling with the idea of her being with other men …though unaware of the knowledge he had of them. This was part of that give and take, the "tit for tat," of the relationship where she gave him something he couldn't get elsewhere …but rightfully expected something of equal value in return. Besides, like a good spanking, the redness would be gone by daylight …and his *fever* broken.

This evening's experience hadn't been to her liking however, it was not what she had come for or what she expected of Jake, not his *role* in her play, or the *position* he played on the team so to speak. She would tell him the next morning as she dressed to leave that she hadn't really enjoyed it, that she wasn't really into that *"hardcore shit"* ...or at least not on that occasion, and if he wanted to see her that evening, he would have to change his game plan.

She expressed what her desires and needs were, and if he thought he could handle that she'd give him a call later. Relieved of the *load* he'd been carrying, he didn't need to reply, she would call around 6:00 and they made their plans accordingly. It was a night that would stand out as their masterpiece, their #1 Hit on the charts, people would've paid to watch.

They met at the usual place, Leon's. It had all the trappings of a fake hook-up, you know the kind married couples sometimes arrange to instill a bit of excitement in their relationship. She arrived first, but he wasn't tardy, she just lived closer. They didn't immediately approach each other, yet stood across the room for a time each examining the other as if they had never met, revisiting the initial attraction. They would drive back to her house separately, he had once again come with that hired-hand attitude about him, aware of the work that needed to be done, but now refocused and mindful of the fact there were other contractors bidding for the same job. At this point he was extremely familiar with the house, had now been in it on numerous occasions *...or outside it looking in*, and strangely felt at home. Once again, the traction thing, she would prepare a pallet on the floor.

He understood the importance of the evening, like a lovesick condemned man being served his last meal, it was that intimate opportunity he had requested and was starving for. The *weeds* and *briers* that had blocked this path now properly disposed. He had waited and plotted for months to revisit the emotions she produced in him, the perfection of that initial weekend that life, the circumstances of their situation ...and intruders had soiled in the interim. There was no "spanking the kitty" on this occasion, no rude *slamming* of kitchen screen doors. He would leave no delicate part of her untouched, but gently this time, with love and tenderness, as only someone who truly cares can, like the song says: **"*Who doesn't long for someone to hold, who knows how to love you without being told.*"**

Last night had been about him and what he had needed, the opportunity to exorcise those demons of Tony and her that she didn't even know existed for him. Tonight would be his gift to her, his effort to show his appreciation and love, and in doing so distance and distinguish himself from all others in her life. They began this dance like lovers not strangers, each now quite aware of the other's body. He would take more time in undressing her than she'd taken in getting prepared. Like a Do-It-Yourself striptease, enjoying each inch of her as he revealed it, her excitement growing in the process, until she could no longer wait to *expose* him.

You probably never met a man that brought his own soundtrack with him, but he did, and he could read her body with the knowledge and expertise of a man who had built an instrument, written the song, had arranged its climax and knew she was close to hers. As she began to gasp, the impression of her fingers deep in his back, he took her there slowly, keeping it just out of reach and making her wait, the darkened room thick with lust and anticipation, "you could feel it coming in the air."

She was almost wrestling with him, climbing him like a ladder from beneath in an attempt to get to that *peak* as if suffocating or starving for it, as if she hadn't been there since the last time *he'd* taken her, when with a genuinely sincere confession he whispered, almost unfairly, *"Can you feel how much I desire you?"* Then he brought it home, rang the bell twice *like the postman*, delivered her package, and just like that they melted into one, their bodies becoming indistinguishable one from the next, it wasn't merely physical, it was spiritual,

…and mutually so. He would absorb the moment unlike any other. He had that awareness of its place and value in his life.

She lay there spent, glowing, beautiful, and voluptuous, like a dark haired Marilyn Monroe, beyond satiated. The "do me" girl had gotten done …and properly so. He had *sufficiently* satisfied all her *needs* and then some, and she told him he could have her anyway he wanted, but he already had. In the *"doing"* she had a way of making him glad to be a man that was entirely her own, leaving none of his physical or emotional *desires* unmet. It would be a difficult act for anyone to follow, including them. The time constraints, the absence of opportunities, and stress from outside sources would make it *next* to impossible. Not to mention that expectations after such an encounter can be recipes for disappointment, but both knew they were capable of accomplishing it in that regard and that is often 90% of the equation.

He had once again reestablished himself, **JOB ONE:** complete. He had also eliminated the competition for a while, **JOB TWO:** complete.

And he had definitely caused her some confusion amidst the euphoria of it, but she would have to straighten up and put it out of mind in a hurry because Glen would be home tomorrow. It was going to be difficult to behave as if something hadn't happened. It was of such a magnitude she almost wished she could tell him.

It goes without saying ...most of the time we think of affairs as consisting of two individuals, one or both of which is involved with a spouse or significant other. But there was more than that going on here, and uncertainty as to what it all meant. It would be a valid question to inquire about how he could go so long between the occasions and maintain that level of interest in the woman and even see it intensify, or why she kept defaulting back to him. It was more than just the "*forbidden fruit is the sweetest*" apparently. For better or worse they seem to have found something necessary in each other they couldn't *satisfy* elsewhere. Despite the long periods apart the emotions remained intact, the opposite side of that "out of sight/out of mind" coin being that sometimes "absence makes the heart grow fonder."

But there was a growing hazard amidst, unknown to either of them, but we've seen evidence of it. The man who'd had sex with an abundance of women had never had to share one like this. Sharing implied a degree of possession, and while the woman hadn't given *that* part of herself to him, somewhere during the course of that first weekend at her house he had gotten a thread of the fabric of his being snagged on an end table ...or the sharp edge of the raw emotion, and that "thread," that emotion, had attached him to her, unintentionally yet undeniably so, and this outing had only reinforced it.

But in the romantic physics of it all, for every *action* there is an equal and opposite *reaction* ...and the *strengthening* of that attachment would also serve to make him more *vulnerable* where she was concerned. He had been operating like a well-oiled machine in his personal dealings up until then, and the introduction of that one all-important aspect was like a flock of birds flying into a jet engine. It hadn't brought him down but it had definitely knocked him off-course.

There's a reason it's called *"falling* in love"... It happens unexpectedly, uncontrollably, and sometimes it <u>hurts.</u> As mentioned early on, *"to want something you can't have, to have something you can't keep,"* was part of the initial allure for the man, but it's a pursuit that don't usually end in happiness. The abundance of conflicting emotions and resulting complications of this romantic *time-share* were starting to tax the man. And when it was said he had gone from being *"different"* to being *"weird,"* we aren't far from *"**weird**"* becoming *"**dangerous,**"* ...to himself and others. That "thread" had already begun to unravel, and the weight of events would quicken the pace.

CHAPTER 11

A CRIMINAL CONVERSATION

"Making love," is an overused misstatement, the truth of the matter is you can't "make" it …like a rainbow it simply occurs, a result of the fact all the necessary ingredients are in place, and the circumstances right …then recognized and appreciated afterward …when it has already been **made**. A natural byproduct of <u>shared</u> emotion that happens all on its own …*or doesn't.*

And it had happened, they'd *made* it, and both of them had felt it. But like two willing participants in an unethical social/sexual experiment, combined in the same situation, having the same experience and the same result …they would have *very* different responses to it. He would revel in it, while she would retreat, a delayed allergic reaction of sorts. As if knowing it was there and she couldn't stay …was worse than never knowing it at all.

And then came the period of dormancy, Jake had come to hate that aspect of the relationship, but it was typical of it from the very beginning. They had spent more time together initially because of the fact that it had begun around the cluster of holidays that had occurred. It was now late May, nearing Memorial Day, his work with Rhonda winding down as his lawn work was in full swing and yet trying to occupy his time in other means, with other women, to keep from going insane, but like a toothache she was never far from his thoughts. Rhonda had sent him to a one-day seminar to get a certificate in online-investigation, they're called MCLE credits, or Minimum Continuing Legal Education credits. Essentially it allowed her to charge more for Jake's services, and he subsequently got a little more himself.

He was already relatively proficient at some of the generic aspects of the course, though it was largely geared towards finding people's hidden assets, and much more in-depth stuff than her clientele required, the biggest thing Jake did for her was find her clients, and they often didn't leave much of an electronic footprint, but the knowledge would prove helpful, as it came with some database accesses he would use to try and learn a bit more about some of these men Rae was communicating with. He was also extremely familiar with the courthouse and how to use the criminal and civil record databases, and he thoroughly looked into everyone he could identify ...who was local. He had routinely done background checks on everyone his ex-wife had been involved with, anyone who would potentially be involved in his son's life, and he extended that concern to Rae.

A couple of the men had been helpful by providing their phone numbers in the emails, some he just had a first name, some he had both as part of their electronic signature, or their actual email addresses, like his own, a combination of initials and name. There were obviously other means of contact, since Tony was not among them, but he knew Tony's name and address, and had eliminated him as a threat, and hopefully, as a competitor through his stunt at the bar, not to mention the way he had taken care of *business* at Easter. Tony was pulling a lot of young leg anyway, and he thought Rae was hot ...but in a "hot for her age" kinda way.

He began by doing Internet searches of all the email addresses, looking to find perhaps a listing on *ebay*, or *craigslist*. Checking ISP addresses in an effort to identify geographic areas, and reverse phone number look-up search engines. It was helpful ...if you can call finding that sort of information about men who want to sleep with a woman you love helpful. The police generally had a low opinion of unlicensed investigators like himself, but he knew a couple who had children that played ball in the same league as his son, and he occasionally enlisted their help with stuff such as running license plates, asking advice, etc., and running names through their databases every time his son's mother changed partners. He would enlist their help under similar premises where Rae was concerned, not to mention he was riding by her house with the frequency of a private security guard, even borrowing Chunk's truck on occasion to avoid the off chance she might recognize his.

He did it in part out of a desire to better understand what she was looking for, what she found attractive about each man, but also to make sure she was safe and that there weren't any unsavory types in the bunch. Two men of interest showed up in the emails. Rae and Vincent had history, or so their communications would suggest, he appeared to be one of the men she *landed* on when she'd previously "fallen" outside the marriage. Jake found his profile on one of the social networks, created a fake account and sent him a friend request pretending to be a guy he went to college with. It worked, and once he had access to the guy's profile, he found him to be, like Tony, relatively harmless. But one guy raised the hair on the dawg's back, and that was William Barry.

William Barry was a bad man. He was that good-looking bastard that the rest of us men hate. He could read women, their weaknesses, their sensitivities, and he used it to his advantage. The type of man who could beat a woman, and have her *apologize* as if she had it coming. And he had done just that, and somehow his name popped up in Rae's inbox. The guy had been kind enough to include a couple of photos, the kind of profile pictures the dating websites discourage you from posting, his body littered with tattoo's of the jailhouse variety. He had also included his phone number, a 704 area code, a reverse-lookup of which came up with nothing, it was obviously a cell number, but concerned, Jake performed a North Carolina Department of Corrections Offender search and found he had a small list of convictions, but they were of a nature that worried him... Drug Possession; done time: **Assault on a Female;** done time ...served 44 months, and while he had been out of jail for a couple of years now, that last one was the sort of crime that doesn't happen as a mistake, Jake thought. It represented a flaw in a man's character with a high rate of recidivism, and somehow he had managed to get into Rae's life.

She had met him through her father's church, volunteering for a community outreach helping revitalize a part of southeast Raleigh for lower income families, and he was working construction. She had the ability to turn her apparent *lack of attention* on and off like a faucet when she found someone she wanted to take notice, and like a predator he sensed her hemorrhaging *neediness*. There was a reference to some upcoming availability in the email she had sent. So using the woman's email account he'd been visiting daily for the past four months he wrote the man, following her note with another accelerating the date and arranging a meeting, and then of course erased any evidence of its existence and its subsequent reply. He had concocted a plan to intervene and discourage the suitor. In a manner of speaking, it was a plan that was about as logical and ridiculous as a female astronaut strapping on an adult diaper and driving cross-country to kidnap and potentially kill a rival for her lover's affections, but ridiculous enough that it might in fact work.

He got there before the agreed upon time to avoid missing him or drawing unnecessary attention to himself, that *psychasthenia* thing perhaps. He thought he recognized Barry, he was a big fucker too, a product of the Tarheel state's prison yard workout facilities, and all kinds of imaginary nastiness was going through Jake's head. Maybe we should be providing inmates something other than free weights to make themselves more menacing Jake pondered. He appeared to be a generous man, as in he was *giving* it in prison, and someone else was on the receiving end. He had the man's phone number, and using a prepaid phone card he'd purchased with cash at the Western Union near Rhonda's office, he gave the man a call so he could identify him for certain before hanging up.

He watched as the fella had a number of drinks, ignored the attention of a few local patrons, and continued glancing at his phone, the "Unknown Caller" ID of the phone card origin prohibiting him from returning the call, not knowing of the ruse or the fact that she was never coming. After an hour or so he appeared to have grown frustrated and tired of waiting, squared his bill, and left. Plan in motion, Jake followed and placed the call to 911 before he deliberately bumped into him at a "Stop" sign just minutes from the bar, slight enough to do minimal damage, but enough to require an introduction.

He knew the man was on probation, and hoped to delay him with the necessary exchange of contact info until the police arrived, DWI=probation violation, hopefully revocation… go directly to jail, do not pass "GO" or collect on Mrs. Johnston's offer. But there was an unusual uneasiness about the man, Jake sensed the apprehension about him, and as he returned to his car *"to get his registration and insurance info,"* Jake followed him.

He had recognized Jake from the bar, and apparently had some cause for concern, an understandable aversion to returning to prison perhaps, as mentioned earlier, sometimes the *strong* become the *prey* in certain circumstances, and with his left leg on the ground outside the vehicle, his right on the floorboard as he leaned across the front seat and opened the glove box, it wasn't papers but a flash of *gun-barrel* blue that he pulled from the compartment. This ain't happening Jake thought to himself, and in an *Oh-My-God* moment, he kicked the door shut on the man's extended leg, heard the crack of the bone, the man dropped the flashlight, …that's right it was a flashlight, and not a pistol. Dragged his broken shin into the car, slammed the door and sped away.

What the fuck? Aside from the concern he had unjustly broken the man's leg, the bastard had driven away. All manners of questions were running through his mind as he ran back to his truck and proceeded to chase the man. It had the atmosphere of a scene from the **Matrix**, everything seemingly happening in slow motion, except for his racing thoughts. The absurdity of the moment didn't escape him, like the episode from the show *The Soprano's* where Paulie and Christopher drive to the "pine barrens" to bury the body of the Russian mobster they had "killed" only to open the trunk and have the man jump out and flee and find themselves chasing him blindly through the darkness of the New Jersey forest.

In a similar vein he was now pursuing a man whom he had rear-ended ...intentionally, after forewarning the police, a man whose leg he had broken because he was getting a flashlight from the glove box. The thought of bailing crossed his mind as he kept the dispatcher updated on their whereabouts, but there was a high degree of possibility that might make things worse. It must've been like that period of time between when the suicidal man steps from the ledge and kisses the pavement, a conversation with himself contemplating his decision all the way down, all of which was moot. The plan had begun as a humanitarian effort, it was teed up to be potentially heroic, albeit unknown and undetectable, like a SEAL Team 6 operation, but it was quickly evolving into **"Black Hawk Down"** and looking more likely that he might have gotten involuntarily committed ...or arrested as the case turned out to be.

Jake had kept 911 abreast of their location, an awkward conversation to be sure, and eventually RPD corralled Barry into an office building parking lot, his car crippled as he tried to jump the curb and drive off through the woods.   Jake followed excitedly like *Gomer Pyle* making a citizen's arrest, his behavior wasn't easily understandable, ...but inexplicable wasn't a crime.   Leaving the scene of an accident, assault, and DWI however were. Rhonda was the first call he made, and she met him at the Wake County Detention Center.   Barry had been arrested, "Thank God," DWI and drugs in the car, and after his wounds were tended to, it would be enough to send him back to prison.   At least he would no longer be a variable in their equation, and more importantly no threat to Rae.   But Jake was now one of Wake County's ***Slammer Magazine*** thumbnails ...alongside William Barry, and he couldn't even tell her the why of it all.   It was a dangerous time to be lovers apparently.

Though they had been in contact on a daily/weekly basis, it had now been four weeks since he'd *plowed her flowerbed* at Easter, and Rae was the **second** call he made, waiting until after he was back at home the next morning and she had taken the children to school. He obviously left the details out, telling her only that he had gotten the DWI. She said she was "worried sick" about him and would pay him a visit that coming weekend, after all he was a captive audience, in North Carolina you automatically lose your license for ten days following a DWI arrest.

He recognized the tone of her voice though, it was the tone she often used when she spoke about Glen, of indifference and detachment as if she took some obscene pleasure in the man's difficulties because they stood as a reminder of how good she had it. He thought he could hear her smiling at the news, perhaps not overtly, but like she had when she first saw him that October night at Leon's, unaware of it herself, and that genuineness made it all the more unpalatable. As if she thought the universe had a finite amount of misfortune and the more that befell him, the less likely it was to visit her. He still wanted to see her though and would write her in the interim, it went something like this:

What can I say? You wrote me once very early on that you *"want a relationship of total openness and honesty because I know that commitment will come naturally and freely from such an approach."* However, it takes two to make this happen. Commitment, that's a scary word, kinda like stress. I've avoided it as much as I could ;)) ...it implies responsibility, and we both have our share of those, especially you.

But only moments have no strings Rae, ...relationships, friendships, (the good ones at least) cannot escape them or they have no true value, or strength. Would you trust yourself to drive across a bridge that wasn't sound? Honesty, openness, acceptance, ...trust, are all strings of varying lengths, and widths.

I know you've got other interests. But you are showing me that you recognize the value of our friendship, and are caring for it when I need it most. You've said it several times, "Actions speak louder than words"... and I know it sounds like I'm writing this past-tense, but knowing that you'll be coming, and that you want to be here for me, is keeping me from "falling apart"... until I can "fall apart" safely with you. I'm continuing to find "positives" that are arising out of this "shit" that I stepped in, and the fact that our friendship will inevitably be stronger because of it is one I hold dear. If I were writing this on a piece of stationary, it would have a tear stain now.

I am aching for Saturday. As always...I will be here if you need me ...even if I have to take a cab ;) ...and I say this sincerely my friend, as never before...

Love,

-Jake

It sounded overdramatic and it was, but it was incomplete, some of the more important details missing, like telling someone you had a kidney removed, but being incapable of telling them you had given it to them. But she never made it anyway, swing and a miss… "Strike two." Love may not keep score, but what about friendship? Just as the evidence was mounting to make a case for the lack of it, so was his desire and determination to prove otherwise.

As for Rhonda and Chunk, he had some explaining to do, but his mind was somewhere else. The disappointment hidden by failed attempts at humor, and for the first time in the relationship he had that moment where he had to face the reality that she was more important in his life than he was in hers. He had known it was there but had been able to avoid looking at it because it lacked any detriment.

He understood that try as you might, you can't convince someone to feel something they're not naturally inclined to, but emotion was the constant in his equation with her, not the variable, and he couldn't take it out. Like some thesis for his Psych major he was *deducing* from his years of experience with women, narrowing it down to a specificity towards her, and in so doing placing great significance on it. She conversely was *inducing* from her experience with him and applying it broadly to others, and thereby denying any significance. Perhaps it in fact had none for her, or perhaps, she had to behave as if it had none in order to complete the task of raising her kids as she saw it, at Glen's expense.

They were in a romantic Catch-22, she a long way from the finish line, and his patience was not that patient. The relationship was an island in both their lives; however for him it was a destination, for her it was a layover, an airport hub to other destinations, but he had proven he could manipulate her situation so that she had fewer choices and *flights*, thereby maintaining his value to her.

He had danced around their verbal agreement like a tax lawyer looking for loopholes. He hadn't directly stepped in her business with Tony he rationalized ...only tossed a number of rocks over the proverbial fence. Though it's <u>doubtful</u> the woman would've agreed. Even this disaster with Barry had taken place outside her perimeter as he saw it. But he was about to trespass, to act instead of react. He told himself he was doing it for her sake, and he truly believed it.

A church near where he lived had a saying on the sign out front that read: "What angers you controls you." He'd remembered that one, he had found it to be true in his life. As consumed as he could be with things, anger was difficult to let go of, and his anger was like a pinball, while he could batter it around and forget about it for a time with the wonderful distractions of his son and their life together, work, and his friends, like the pinball, it always returned to the hole at the bottom of the table, he could not dispose of, nor ignore it.

The man who had purposely avoided serious relationships was now involved with a married woman, a married woman who was sleeping with other men besides her husband, *besides him* ...and that's a hard mouthful for any man to swallow.

To love someone, and know that was going on is contrary to a man's nature, ...that bears repeating, for a man to love a woman as he seemed to, and know what was going on and put up with it, to have seen it with his own eyes, is contrary to a man's nature. While it has all the appearance of a weakness or lack of self-respect, it must've taken an incredible strength. His tolerance as such would wear thin, but not out. A product of his competitive nature, and the notion he could win her over. But there's no pride or blue ribbon to be had in the "stomaching that plate of shit" contest...

People don't walk into obsession, they find themselves there, and as a matter of self-preservation, upon that finding, they sometimes have to deny it. To be aware you are in denial is to *not* be in denial. How fucked up is that? But he would eventually say he wasn't denying it, just not acknowledging it. Rhonda and Chunk knew something was up with the man, but he wasn't volunteering information. Rhonda wasn't one to refrain from stating the obvious though, and she would inquire about his love life. He would tell her not to worry, that she was still number one in his heart, as she then told the boy to hush and informed him that women *"ate men like him"* where she came from. *"I'm not a barbeque sandwich,"* he reminded her lovingly.

It was about this time he began to reveal elements of what was going on to his friends, never revealing much though, they would only come to know her as the *"married girl."* It all began to make some sense, the polarities in his behavior, the spring in his step, and the periods of distant preoccupation. This had been going on for seven months and he hadn't made nary a suggestion of it, partly because he knew he would not have an agreeable audience with his two friends, and mostly to protect the woman, *the married girl.* It took something like this to get him to open up vaguely.

Jake couldn't explain the woman's behavior, and he tried. He had obviously ignited something in her, and it had quickly become a wildfire and made of him an ill-equipped makeshift smokejumper starting *backfires* to contain the blaze. Unaware to her, and much to her dislike, a marginally effective invisible cockblocker, or box-blocker as the gender may be.

He wasn't just trying desperately to funnel all the action his way, but to protect her. "Goddamn woman ...why can't she just behave?" he wondered. It was probably somewhere about here on this trek, in a moment of honesty with himself, he had to admit he wished he'd lifted her from the marriage when she'd come to that brink and he had the chance. In retrospect it didn't seem conscionable *but* cowardly. You should never start something you don't have the courage or heart to finish.

He would give his attorney friend the background info on William Barry, not how or why he knew it though. Rhonda would get the assault charges dropped, Barry's record, despite Jake's *supposed* unawareness of it, made him a perceivable threat, and therefore his actions deemed reasonable in that regard. The "leaving the scene" went away as well, but the DWI charge would stick since Jake was at the legal limit, and that alone would have serious consequences and financial ramifications for the self-employed single-dad. Rhonda was rightfully worried about him. He was her guy, and it was unusual behavior for him, and she would tell him in that way only true friends can, not what he wanted to hear, but what he needed to. There is a distinct difference between hearing and listening however, and he **heard** what she had to say he just wasn't **listening**. He would be less forthcoming as well.

Jake was learning the hard way some things about the woman he loved. She was apparently a non-discriminating gal, an equal opportunity adulteress. "I expect she'll sleep with her husband next," he thought. And it was right about this time he gave some consideration to involve the man, why should he be doing all the work? He had Glen's cell phone number, late one night after he'd had a few cold ones he got curious about the man, so he *67'd his number blocking it from display, and called the university directory and got his extension.

It was well past midnight, he knew he wouldn't be there, so he proceeded to dial it, "*Hi you've reached Professor Glen Johnston, and this is the week of... I will be out of the office until Monday, you can leave a message, or if you need to contact me you can reach me on my cell at 919-555-5168,*" Jake made a note of the number, it seemed a waste of potentially valuable info otherwise.

Glen unfortunately sounded like a nice guy over the phone, perhaps they should get together and discuss his wife who was fucking everything insight...or out of sight as it were. Rhonda had a similar message on her phone, and it didn't strike him as unusual. So he had the man's number in case he needed to enlist his help, even if doing so put himself at risk.

North Carolina is one of a few remaining states that still have an *Alienation of Affection* law on the books... we are *steeped in tradition* and stubborn after all... It has its origin rooted in the idea of a spouse as *property*, the loss of which had a negative impact on the household, however in recent times it had become *distorted* in a sense and used to punish infidelity and avenge one's assaulted ego, though extremely rare ...like making a public admission of inadequacy. Its not a criminal offense, but a tort, a civil action that allows a spouse to seek damages against a third party whose conduct deprived the husband or wife filing the action of the love and affection that previously existed between husband/wife and his/her spouse.

Now there's room for debate about whether that previously existed or not, the *preponderance of evidence* leaning towards the "**NOT**"... Jake would argue her affections for Glen Johnston were quite intact ...it was her legs that kept falling apart. If he were guilty of anything it would have been **Criminal Conversation**, or adultery, and if that became an issue or went to trial it was gonna be a *class action* lawsuit.

Unseen, he had all the appearance of a man trying to keep the marriage together, but Glen wasn't doing his part, and Jake thought it time to share the burden. "I'll send him a text," he thought, it would need to sound like it came from a woman, ambiguous and vague as to who specifically it was regarding, only give him reason to take a closer look at his wife, and in the process, *once again*, hamper her scamper, stomp her romp.

Jake knew all about disposable cells, he was always bumping up against them trying to catch up to people in his Investigator role with Rhonda, while her reputation and clientele had improved over the years, she had not abandoned her original bread and butter. Respected and popular with the population of defendants charged with DWI and drug arrests, those who often need help but can't afford it. She was afforded the proper respect on the street because of the openness of her heart for such cases, but a few of them often repaid her kindness with skipping on the bill, and Jake spent a portion of his time trying to track them down to garnish wages, or work out payment arrangements, and would often receive a percentage of what he recovered as a result.

He knew how to find people who didn't want to be found, and often frequented the parts of town the police don't go alone in an effort to do so. As her agent, he had his own street-cred as well because he was fair, and while he could be an asshole when the situation demanded, he wasn't unnecessarily an uncompromising hard-ass. He had such a phone he had purchased with cash several months ago, long enough that any store surveillance would have routinely been written over ...though the place he bought it in southeast Raleigh, probably only had the cameras for appearance.

He asked a random young woman to leave a message on the phone, coaching her along, it said:

"Hi, sorry I missed your call, leave me an interesting message and I'll get back to you. Bye Now."

His original intent was that he would use it at some point to communicate with Rae so that nobody could tie them together. That way if Glen tried to call back he'd get the woman's voice, and the phone would have long been gone, it was after all disposable ...not an original idea, your fifteen your-old could be doing it, but it's effective and it happens everyday. But what would he say in the text?

The more he thought about it, the more he thought he might be better served to send it to Rae instead, after all he didn't want to completely eliminate her activities, just his rivals. And while he'd literally laid the man's wife out on their dinner table and *stuffed* her like a Thanksgiving turkey, strange as it may sound he didn't want to hurt Glen's feelings, knowledge might be power ...but ignorance **is** bliss.

What you don't know can't hurt you ...*or so they say*, and as long as she was married she'd still have need of him he reasoned ...his *ir*-rationale no different than her *justifiable adultery.* So he sent Rae the text. What it said was unimportant, only that she got the *message* that someone knew about her extramarital *activities* so to speak, and she received it as evidenced by the equally spiteful response. She wasn't a woman to be bullied or run from a fight either... And the disposable phone became *disposed.*

It seemed that the things that made them different from other folks might have been what they had most in common, like water and ice, two states of the same substance. Unable to coexist for any length of time before evolving into one or the other, one of them having to concede and undoubtedly making a mess in the process. And it seemed he was *dissolving.* She may have been a prisoner of her circumstances, but she was the *"shot caller"* in the prison yard of <u>this</u> relationship. And while he had been successful in editing her visitors list, when all was said and done ...*she* still had the final say in who she would entertain.

He was and is a great guy …honestly, but she had *diluted* him. It wasn't anything time wouldn't take care of, but right now he wasn't himself, and neither Chunk nor Rhonda knew all that entailed. At forty-five he was on a spiritual/emotional/sexual scavenger hunt it seemed and she represented a lot of the things on his list. There were others out there that would've "fit the bill" of course …but he'd stumbled onto her pretty ass and taken a liking to what he'd *found* …and *lost* his mind in the process.

CHAPTER 12

A STORM IN A TEACUP

It was now July, and that North Carolina asphalt was getting hot...

He hadn't lain down with *her* since he'd sent the text. Like a *friendly-fire* incident, it was an undesirable but unavoidable casualty and consequence of the decision. His actions following the business with William Barry had cleared the bench to be sure, but also made her rightfully cautious and left him a bit in the dark as she had abandoned the email account upon the scare.

He had always been able to tell when she'd been busy ...or planned to be, even when it wasn't publicized in her email. She had an unmistakable hesitation in her voice and gaps between her words, probably because she had already discovered it difficult to lie to the man. He now recognized the visual that went with it as he watched her approach, her steps unsteady like those of someone who knows they're being watched and scrutinized, as though she was having to think about each one, an impromptu model's first strut down the runway or a baby's first steps. Did he know about her activities, the lies she had told him beyond Tony? And if he did, was he fucking with her... After the now routine socially acceptable public display of affection, she sat down across from him. It had to be reminiscent of two spies sitting down together, each believing they knew something the other didn't, and neither knowing as much as they thought, and yet a strange codependency and trust existed because each had *something* the other coveted.

If we were to retrace his steps, he had hacked her email, faked an STD, called the police because she had "*company*," fucked her brains out, gone so far as to deliberately cause an accident with a felon on probation in an effort to thwart her plans to get together with the man, not to mention broken the bastard's leg and gotten arrested, and then sent her an ambiguous untraceable text shaking her life up and not left any footprints to speak of. All while the images and imaginings of these other men she didn't know he knew about were rattling around in his uneasy thoughts. These are generally not considered the actions of a balanced mind. The man was literally *Missing In Action*, the "lights were on" as they say, but "nobody was home," probably off somewhere *unraveling...* And yet he could still sit across from her, a warm, loving quizzical smile of the boy-next-door variety on his face, indicative of the fact he knew her well enough to know something was on her mind, but leaving the responsibility of what it was for her to say *...because he already knew*. Leaving the poor woman with the uneasiness that she had done something she didn't want him to know about. It was disturbing, deceptive and cold, in psychological terms they call it *"fuckin' nuts,"*...or a **Young & The Restless** storyline.

She would tell him about the anonymous message she had gotten, concerned and suspicious of its origin, judging his reaction to the news, but unconcerned that he might've sent it ...it had placed him front and center of the bull's-eye, it was illogical that he would, but that was the intent. She would only inquire about anyone in his life who might have reason to be jealous... It could not have been more "**ironic.**"

His demeanor was enough for her to scratch him off any list of potential authors. She never asked him anything like you might expect, and he would never lie to her. On some level she must have simply decided she didn't really want to know, the answer potentially more unsettling than the question and uncertainty. And once having decided not to go there, the meeting took its usual course, an informal therapy session where she would proceed to tell him all about her woes, and get her *"ego-boost"* prescription refilled before its conclusion. He would never meet anyone who had such a low self-esteem, yet high opinion of her self.

He knew of Glen's father's passing, she had called him as soon as she got the news, driving the Suburban and the kids to Norfolk for the funeral, Glen already there. It now seemed his mother who had early onset Alzheimer's might be coming to live with them. The woman, he learned, had an uncanny knack for stating the obvious, and saying the very thing that every one else was thinking but afraid to.

Rae confessed the woman had never liked her, nor the fact that Glen had married a woman with her *baggage,* and she was convinced the dementia had given her a license so to speak, and she was conveniently using her intermittent *episodes* as an excuse to say things she otherwise might not have ...mean things, calling her a "*gold digger*" and a "*tramp,*" and Jake would just shake his head at the *audacity* of the woman ...Rae, not the mother. And just like his body would tense at the sound of the dentist's drill, he braced himself, clutching the arms of the chair when her conversation headed down this painful path... It was part of the deal, that necessary role he'd accepted to maintain his place in her life, but who in God's name would have wanted it other than him.

The way he described it made it sound like emotional water-boarding, a torturous but necessary chore, and he performed it every time the opportunity presented itself, but it was less frequent that he'd get the *cookie* he desired and was promised, that *nookie*. Over time the cumulative inequity of that aspect of their arrangement began to cause him some irritability, he was noticeably getting a bit ornery. No two ways about it, he was fit to be tied ...and perhaps he should have been. Two bulls will sometimes bump heads when there ain't a female in the pasture ...it's rather playful actually, but you add one *heifer* to the mix and somebody's feelings *usually* get *hurt*...

He didn't need a designated driver, he just needed **a** driver, now having a restricted license because of the DWI. In reality it was equal parts about getting out of the house on a Friday night, and an excuse to get together with his buddy, he and Chunk hadn't seen each other much of late. And while he hadn't said as much, he hadn't gotten any pussy lately, and the dawg, that beast, needed to be fed, and the *asshole* knew he looked good standing next to his round friend. He hadn't seen Tony's GTO parked off in the corner of the lot, under a streetlight and occupying two spaces in an arrogant but understandable attempt to avoid any dings, otherwise they may have likely gone elsewhere.

It was unclear as to what sparked the interaction between the two men, as if they started in the middle of something previously heated and unfinished of an impolite and disrespectful nature. Our man seemed an unwilling participant if that counts for anything. His attempts at barstool diplomacy failing though, and before he could finish his beer, he was telling Chunk he needed to step outside. He had thrown the vibe out there a few months back when he was "feeling" it, and now it was coming back to him at a time when he wasn't …but like a fart in church, he'd have to own it. The boy who had never learned to run from trouble was now a middle-aged man incapable of it.

He was looking annoyed as if it was petty and avoidable business. To be honest he didn't want any trouble with the young man at this point. He might not have cut him from the team, but he had cleverly made certain he wasn't getting much playing time, and he feared any drama of a Jake/Tony sort would get back to Rae and before long she'd connect some unattractive dots. The instigator however, had said something derogatory to him, mixed with something unflattering about the aforementioned female, pissed him off, and wouldn't ease up when given the chance.

Chunk tagged along because he had Jake's back and all, but was noticeably a little worried ...*because he had Jake's back and all...* They say water don't flow up hill, and shit rolls down hill, and a guy called "Chunk" probably can't fight *nor* run too damn well, but they were best friends and to his credit he was prepared to take a beating for his pal if need be, or at least get in the way of one, 'cause he knew the man would do the same for him. Jake was starting to tremble, the *"static"* showing up like a bothersome in-law uninvited, the untimely pimple he would sometimes get, but his friend had never been a witness to it in all the time he'd known him. The sight of this roughneck bastard/soccer-dad that would be bringing snacks and juice boxes to the game in the morning *appearing* nervous made Chunk nervous as well, like a yawn ...it was contagious.

Jake had done his due diligence ahead of time, took measure of the young man so to speak. Which hand did he favor, was he calm and confident, *too* calm and *over*confident for the man he was like he might have an *accessory*. By the time they got to the parking lot the *static* had him shaking like Kevin Bacon in the **Hollow Man**, as if caught transitioning between two realities, one visible and one unseen, …and in a sense he was, his *invisible man* struggling with the one the people in his daily life *saw* and it gave him the appearance of being nervous when he wasn't, only a *live-wire* now instead.

"What's the matter old man, you afraid?" asked Tony snidely. *"Actually I am. I'm afraid I'm going to harm you."* Jake strained as though confessing to a crime he hadn't yet committed and already remorseful. Not the answer Tony expected, and one he didn't have a ready reply for. Then solemnly, as though he saw himself going some place he'd been before and not really wanting to go back there, Jake inquired, *"If I hurt you will you promise not to press charges?"* The response was an abbreviated chuckle and dismissive *"You gotta be fuckin' kidding me?"* with a smart-assed smirk. *"Nope …not 'fuckin' kidding.' I hope you have some kinda insurance."* Jake finished. Then before the boy could get the

puzzled shit-eating grin off his face the forty-five year-old hit the twenty-eight year-old, not once but twice, and they were the sorta blows that made the handful of bystanders that had gathered collectively wince. The first knocking the man off balance, then stepping towards him as if tracking his descent, an abrupt second, *much* harder than the first, born out of "*pure meanness*" laying him flat out, poised momentarily for an unnecessary third before slowly pulling it back like a gunslinger holstering his weapon.

Felled like a tree, Tony lay there unable to get up, looking for a tooth, his shit, or some evidence of where he was. And then Jake straddled him in his incapacity, paused above him as though he'd finally become angry, and in a *veni, vidi, vici* moment, pulled out his cock and proceeded to piss on him ...in front of God and everyone as if oblivious to the small crowd. And no one dared to remind him. He then knelt and whispered something to the boy, and as he stood, reached into his left pocket and turned it inside out, emptying a small measure of sand or *salt* on the ground in the process before tucking it back in like he'd been at the beach for the day.

It was humiliating, degrading, and "yeah," gratifying in that fucked up way seeing someone get what they had coming is, a *Roman holiday*... The baddest sequence of events Chunk would ever witness, like a scene from a Tarantino or Scorsese movie only in real-life. He'd have applauded but he was simultaneously shocked and worried, and shocked... But he could testify with some certainty that it is definitely better to be *"pissed off"* than pissed on. He had thought his friend capable of it, he now knew him to be, and that's an important distinction among men, between what you *think* and what you *know*, between what you *know* and what you can _prove_. Chunk knew one damn thing, if he ever saw the man start to rattle like that again he was gonna give him a lotta space, and a sufficient amount of time to throttle down. Goddamn motherfucker.

It happened impressively fast, like flashes from a gun barrel, and frighteningly vicious, unlike the man he knew, as if the *static* that had built up in the preceding months had discharged all over the boy's face. Condensed yet violent, it was like a *storm in a teacup*. And in the resulting calm that follows such a force of nature, Jake had the appearance of simply being inconvenienced and a look of buyer's remorse at the expenditure of one of those dwindling and valuable *kick ass* "rain-checks," he'd been holding onto ...like he had been forced to use a gift-card he was saving to buy something nice for his son to purchase a toilet instead.

He went and leaned against Chunk's diesel and waited for the inevitable sirens and side-effects that would follow, threw his arm over his friend's shoulder as if *comforting* him in *his* nervous state, and politely asked him to call Rhonda, the attorney's dear friend disturbingly becoming a regular client. Chunk was still processing it all like he'd just been in a damn car wreck, "*What'd you whisper to that guy Dawg?*" he asked, "*I told him how to get that stain out,*" he replied with a wink.

They say you can make a nice dog mean, but not a mean dog nice, you can make it obey ...but not nice. Jake Arnett is a nice guy, but Chunk had seen a side of his friend that he hadn't in the half a lifetime he'd known him. Apparently you can remove the dog from the fight, but not the fight from the dawg, and the marriage of nature and nurture had bred him as such. And in a life-lesson learned, Tony now had a stenciled image in his mind of what a dangerous man might look like.

There was something underlying it all though, some emotions *shaking the pin loose*, kicking him in the side, and making him mean. "That *married girl*" is all he'd say, and Chunk knew not to ask more. His friend would tell him when he was good and ready. Then Jake proceeded to ask him, "*What's up with this old man shit? That's the second time someone has said that to me,*" a reference to Olivia, which Chunk knew nothing of at the time. "*I like the gray aesthetically, it looks good on me,*" he continued, "*but I don't particularly like the reactions I'm getting to it. Whadda you think Chunk?*"

"*I'm not feeling particularly disagreeable pal,*" Chunk confessed. "*I think it was an asset tonight, that fella didn't know what hit him.*" Then Jake looked at him and grinned, revealing a glimpse of the kid he was when they'd met and become friends twenty-three years before, his eyes smiling yet damp. "*You got that right*" he said, but his thoughts were already migrating elsewhere, toward his son, his predicament, and ultimately towards her.

While it probably wound up an inconspicuous YouTube video, everything does these days, nothing more became of it. Jake told Rhonda how to prepare his defense just as he had with the recent fiasco with Barry. Most of the witnesses questioned would state Jake had been put in a defensive posture, prefaced his actions with a disclaimer of sorts and acted reluctantly, sorta, up until the potty business. In the end Tony wouldn't press charges, after the literal and figurative swelling went down he rightfully concluded Jake had more facts than assumptions where he and Rae were concerned, and more than a casual interest in it. Pressing charges would only open him up to injuries of a different sort and cause him greater difficulties ...and he liked his job and the ladies at the Club. He wouldn't know what to tell the woman anyway, and pride would've prohibited him from describing to her how he'd gotten his ass kicked, or what he could remember of it. It's doubtful he ever saw the woman naked again though ...some things aren't worth the price you have to pay for them.

CHAPTER 13

A LIMA BEAN IN A DIXIE CUP

Please forgive the gaps in our story, we are not "losing time." The affair was likened to a crack addiction, episodic and characterized by brief intense highs, and long periods of uneasiness and restlessness in between opportunities while waiting for the next "hit" or "dose," and this was never a Jack and Jill story, or even a little ditty about "Jack and Diane" for those old enough to appreciate the reference. You might think there were no ordinary or mundane aspects of their lives, though make no mistake they were there, but irrelevant to what was foremost at the very beginning of this journey, …that this was a love story, atypical, but a love story nonetheless, and it is about to get a bit more complicated.

It's now late summer, early September to be more precise, and North Carolina summers can be long and relentless, the enthusiasm they begin with fading in the monotonous and oppressive heat. August still only had 31 days, but it had dragged on like a long slow southern drawl leaving the inhabitants parched and ready for the change of seasons, and September brought that promise with it. Like the transition from summer to fall, this period in our story is similarly *active*.

There had been no drought this year. But the rain came infrequent like their encounters, in brief downpours and often accompanied by storms. It had been polite enough to fall in the evenings and Sundays so as not to impede his work, but it was only enough to keep things from drying up all together. Similarly, there had been an inadequate quantity of Raen for his needs. With children out of school their opportunity for sexual encounters had been reduced to sporadic, spontaneous and brief, often *uncomfortable* visits, neither really getting their fill.

They got together often enough, mostly for coffee or a beer in the late afternoons, it satisfied part of her appetite, but for Jake it was like continually visiting the beach and never getting in the water, he was desperate to get wet. And he knew just the spot. When a hunter finds a location where he has had a lot of success, he frequents it, sometimes even builds a blind, or puts up a deer stand so that he can revisit it without the trouble of having to do so again and again. Fishermen who have a similar success return to that cove, or hidden pond for the same purposes. The "Creek," like Leon's had been such a spot for Jake.

Relatively speaking, he was probably batting .250 at the Crooked Creek this season, and he returned, like the fisherman, the hunter, in hopes of landing one. He would meet someone who would challenge his relationship with Rae, a keeper, someone who was his equal in some ways, and exceeded him in others. Her name was Nicole. Dark hair, dark eyes, a full-blooded Seminole, she wasn't just beautiful, she was mysterious and sexy. At forty years of age she was properly inflated, not a wrinkle on her. In many respects she was the female equivalent of Jake. If people were numbered so that we could readily identify members of the opposite sex we're compatible with ...they were a pair. He asked her if he could buy her another beer as she stood holding an empty longneck like a prop, but there was the implication he was looking to quench his own thirst, and she was a long cool drink. He wouldn't bed her that first night, or the second. Not because she didn't want him to, but because she did, but she wasn't a one-night stand, and he was gonna have to prove his worth. The chemistry was evident. They went together like *slow* and *steady*.

She lived in Archer Lodge, a small community in Johnston County. Divorced within the past two years, she had moved to North Carolina from Florida when her son had enrolled at an area university, she had a daughter who was a couple of years older than Jake's boy. She was the kind of woman that the silence was never awkward or uncomfortable, and that alone made her unique. When she finally let him undress her, it was one of those events he'd remember. The Native American could ride like a *reverse cowgirl*, and when she *came* it was like a stone skipping across the water, the orgasms rolling one into the next, growing in intensity and closer together before the final sinking plunge. Like watching the sunset, you could see it disappearing on the horizon, and then it was gone, and beautifully so.

"I'm gonna call you pebble," he said grinning, *"Because...?"* she asked. Not wanting to tell her the real reason for fear it would inhibit her, *"Because you've aged well,"* he laughed. She thought to hit him, but then he followed the quip with a more acceptable explanation, *"because you're cool and smooth, and you haven't allowed life to make you jagged."* *"If I'm pebble, I guess that makes you rock,"* she responded, tugging at his *hardness.* *"Rolling stone might be more accurate,"* he confessed. *"How 'bout you just call me 'again'?"* he said. *"How 'bout I just call you 'often'?"* was the reply.

She liked the man, he was strong enough to be gentle. Beyond the literal implication that he was physically strong enough to be gentle in *handling* her, but in that sense he was secure enough in his manhood that he didn't need to posture or pose as such, and it allowed him to be tender. She was right there, in his life, unencumbered, uncomplicated and available, but he wasn't, not in the way she needed him to be. He had approached it from the very beginning like every other occasion where he had seen a woman more than once, telling her upfront that all he had to offer was friendship, he needed his freedom, and she of course was afforded hers. After all friendship was the firmest foundation of all, and out of it many things can grow, and things began too, but it wasn't long before that emotional claustrophobia reared its ugly head.

By early October they were spending most of their free time together. She could sense there was an obstacle, he hadn't said as much, but he didn't need to, but she was content and not in a hurry, and they would grow closer, or as close as they could. All he knew was that for the first time since the affair had begun he felt an outside draw, it was a confusing time for our man Jake. He'd desire, but perhaps not deserve her, but he wouldn't *play* her either.

He would search himself for reasons not to give in to the relationship, but all he really needed was the one reason …Rae. It was incredibly fucked up to be sure, but not unlike him. He'd heard the proverbial "click," and felt that fateful sensation that accompanies stepping on a landmine, knowing it was going to go off, but not *when* or *whom* it would hurt. It was exactly the sort of situation he had purposely and desperately avoided, yet there he was, quietly stuck between a *pebble* and a hard place.

He hadn't seen Rae in the month since meeting Nicole. It was a busy time for both, children heading back to school, and Glen was around more than usual. Aside from that he had long since learned the proper balance in his communication with her, too much had the effect of creating that appearance of neediness and the resulting apprehension and distance would follow as a consequence. If he waited, she would initiate the contact, and since he had met Nicole he was finding himself ...distracted? He was still hungry for time with Rae, would've made himself available anytime the opportunity arose, but he wasn't starving like he had and she sensed it. Someone else, someone he wasn't talking about had changed the tone of his voice, the *stray* dawg was being fed elsewhere, and it made her insecure. It would seem some women aren't much different than men in the sense that she might not have wanted him for herself as much as she didn't want someone else to have him, she damn sure didn't want to lose him. He was her biggest fan...

The flight from Raleigh to New Orleans went through Charlotte. The airport code on the ticket said MSY, it stood for Moisant Stock Yard, better known as Louis Armstrong International Airport. We all know it by a number of different nicknames, the "Big Easy," "NOLA," "Naw'leans," home to "Fat Tuesday" and Bourbon Street where vice was not only welcomed but *expected*. It was an enchanting, exotic place, one of those few cities in the U. S. where you felt as though you were visiting another country all together. Or at least that's how the boy from North Carolina who had never been further south than Charleston perceived it. The people, the culture, the language ...all *seductive*.

Rae had family there, her mother's side, they weren't native to the area, but longtime residents, and she had also gone as part of an outreach through her father's church. The destruction of Katrina in 2005 had devastated the city, but part of what makes New Orleans special is its resiliency. Geographically it was always vulnerable, like a glass chin on a big-mouth little man daring someone to take a punch, the hurricane had, and the region had not entirely recovered from the blow.

She had been there nearly a week, but before she left Raleigh had invited Jake to come and spend the last weekend with her. In retrospect she must've sensed him drifting and the invitation was an attempt to bring him close again ...and he didn't need much coaxing either. He wouldn't tell Nicole anything other than he was going out of town for a long weekend. It was an asshole thing to do, but all the relationship required of him. He was a follow your heart kind of man and his took him to New Orleans.

He would arrive early Thursday, take a cab to the Bed and Breakfast he had made reservations at, and they would spend the next three days as an ordinary couple, or as ordinary as their circumstances would allow. As difficult as it had been to be apart for those long periods, it can be more difficult to be in close proximity to someone you have such strong feelings for and to have to keep them on a leash, to not allow yourself to act on the affection that seemed so natural. They had the kind of chemistry that's hard not to notice, and the weekend presented the first real opportunity to be uninhibited and not conceal it. He knew what she was in need of, what their relationship was in need of, some space beyond the confines the necessary secrecy of the affair demanded, some romance and intimacy beyond the sex, some semblance of what a normal healthy relationship between a man and a woman looked like. She'd never really had it in her life. It was what it was, and he was intent to make the most of it.

New Orleans was indeed a naughty place. He had done his homework ahead of time and made an informal agenda, his hope to make the occasion special for her, Jazz club, Cajun cuisine, perhaps even a fortune-teller. Part of that agenda also included Scarlett. It had now been a year since that first encounter at Leon's. In that time, among the many things she had confessed and confided to our man, she had expressed her desire to explore a sexual experience with a woman. Jake had noted in her emails a correspondence with an individual named Jamie, and he could never accurately assess the gender but he suspected Jamie was a female simply by the tone, or maybe it was the *pink* font ...but it seemed to have never come to fruition, in part because of the chaos he had created in sending her the text.

She had explained in great detail how she wanted to experience such an encounter with Jake, but their activities were so unpremeditated it didn't allow for the cultivation of a third party, so it had remained a fantasy, and she seemed to have abandoned the idea. But he had never forgotten, and wanted to provide her the opportunity. It was easy enough, escort services in New Orleans were abundant, and he arranged it in advance online.

He knew the type of woman she was attracted to, he'd been a witness to it, Nicole would have been such a woman ...but her river didn't flow in that direction. He knew that for her to thoroughly enjoy herself it needed to be someone attractive, but not more attractive than her ...and someone younger, but not too young, and someone who *could carry on an intelligent conversation...* He found that in Scarlett, a buxom redhead originally from Texas, a graduate student taking a rather extended break from school, now working part-time as an escort for an upscale service in New Orleans who was "*open to couples.*" He anticipated the evening could get a bit too lively for their quaint accommodations at the Inn so he rented a room for the evening at an upscale French Quarter Hotel in advance without her knowledge.

They had hardly gotten out of the room the first day, making up for lost time. Friday, however, it was essential to his script that they get out and see the city. Following their dinner reservations, they proceeded to a Jazz club of some notoriety. It was there that they would meet Scarlett. He would receive a text confirming her arrival but she was hard to miss, he was undoubtedly the luckiest man in the room with the two beauties at his side, *all the worlds a stage, and we are merely players* ...and the scenario that had been discussed played out perfectly.

The whole thing would take place without Rae ever knowing Jake had paid for the woman's company, and it was essential to her taking pleasure in it. He would never forget the wicked grin on her face as she took his hand while he *completed* the redheaded task on the agenda. Nor the look on hers as the woman devoured her, an involuntary pained expression of joy at the moment of climax, "*I love you*" she whimpered, her eyes fixed on the man she wished was someone else, still our man Jake, only that she wished he was someone more than who he was relegated to be in her life. It was erotic, loving …and tragically genuine.

For an ordinary couple such an occasion might have represented a last ditch effort to rekindle something fading, an absence of intimacy or erosion of it, but for these two it was galvanizing. A thing of beauty, and well worth the $800 it cost the hardworking man and for him to have been the first man she would ever experience it with ...priceless. The gift not being in the money it cost but the illusion that it had all happened by chance, and thus the true *gift* lay in the fact she would never know it was a *gift*.

The following day couldn't have been anything other than anti-climatic. We've all been there as the last day of our vacation winds down and we begin to think about our return to the real world. Every great exhale and sigh of relief in life followed by an equally expansive inhale, and the influx of awareness reminding us about the responsibilities and life we are returning to. And so it was for Jake and Rae, melancholic. She had that look about her, the tentativeness of a prisoner on work release who knows that the respite is temporary, the appearance of normalcy an illusion, and they'll have to return to their "cell" shortly. He wanted to fix it for her, but it was beyond him.

They had passed by the fortuneteller's shop several times in the past couple of days, the last item on his agenda. They stood studying their reflection in the large window, Jake clutching her hand like a child clutching his mother's on the first day of school, knowing he would have to let go. She gently squeezing his, aware she could not hold onto him indefinitely, neither wanting to step inside for a glimpse of the future, or seemingly already in possession of the knowledge.

293

The affair would always be like that lima bean in a Dixie cup we all grew in 1st or 2nd grade, excited at the fact that it had emerged from the small amount of soil provided, but confined and constricted, it would never be more than just *a lima bean* in a Dixie cup. And it was apparent to them both, they didn't need a crystal ball, the shop window would suffice. So in lieu of the pretense of some future other than what they both foresaw, they passed on the fortune telling and opted for tattoos instead. It would serve as a symbol of their connection, not the images, but the act, a branding ceremony of secret significance if you will.

He got one he had long ago decided upon, only waited for the proper occasion. It was an *ouroboros*, the image of the snake eating itself. Plato had described such a creature as the first living thing in the universe, entirely self-sufficient and subsisting upon itself. A recurring theme found in some form or variation in nearly every religion and culture, symbolic of rebirth and renewal ...the circle of life, and of life everlasting. But to Jake, it simply looked to him as though the snake was his own worst enemy, devouring himself, the epitome of his experience as he saw it. The tattoo represented an *awareness* of the fact, not a *celebration* of it, and that was what held meaning for the man. A souvenir of the weekend, a postcard of sorts forever inked on his being, draped over his left shoulder it was large and enigmatic like her place in his life.

She was at an internal crossroads, a four-way stop sign in a sense. She didn't want to get something common, and yet what she wanted it to represent, *change*, was especially so. Probably the most common tattoo women get at such a juncture in their lives is a tattoo of a butterfly, symbolizing the emergence and evolution of themselves, coming into their own, but Jake talked her into getting a caterpillar instead. It gave the implication of change, represented the same transformation, only it would leave the mystery of what that *"change"* would look like unanswered. She liked it, and the fact that he understood her so well. A fittingly incomplete circle, it found a home around her belly-button, small and discreetly placed like their relationship, hidden in plain sight. Her children would love it. Glen, like most everything else about his wife, simply wouldn't get it.

The last evening in New Orleans was deliberately casual, like that of a more *traditional* couple. The next morning they would arrive at the airport early enough to get their seat assignments beside one another. But the plane rides home would be quiet and awkward. They had been to that elusive place again, their *Nirvana* …and reminded that they couldn't stay. The voodoo-like spell of the weekend was already wearing off, and the pair would share what amounted to a mutual emotional *hangover*. It seems after the "Big Easy" there was to be an opposite and equally big *uneasy*.

CHAPTER 14

THE EIGHTEEN PERCENT DILEMMA

PLANCK'S LAW...Seeing heat: For increasing temperatures, the visible sequence of radiated colors is: black, red, orange, yellow-white, bluish-white.

...And in a nonscientific, but personal observation, the flame typically burns hottest before it burns out. New Orleans had been **bluish**-white hot, and that meant ...she was already mitigating the significance of the weekend.

If we were to mark ourselves as to where we were on this trek, he had been the man characterized by temporary, disposable relationships, and she was seeking an ongoing no-strings attached sexual relationship. It had evolved to where he was now aspiring to keep their relationship ongoing for as long as possible, and she was facing the growing depression and constant disappointment of living with the reminder it presented of what was missing in her life. Hers was a long row to hoe, and he knew it would not be long before she would be seeking some variety and trying to recreate the sensation with someone other than himself, and it pained him.

He too had seen the future in the reflection of the fortuneteller's window, seen the look on her face... recognized their *Dixie cup*. So what do you do when destinies seem written and ill-fated?... Transplant the lima bean to a bigger pot, fuel the flame, rewrite the ending and create your own destiny ...or at least try. It was time to whip out that *Longfellow* of his and write her a letter. Just because things are the way they are doesn't mean that's the way they have to be...

Rae... I'm touching myself thinking about you right now ;) I pity the girl I meet next... she's got a tough act to follow. But then again, you might be the next act if I have anything to do with it ...not getting moist are you? ;) ...need any "meat" in your diet? I know you like it ...and you know I

want it ;) ...nice things to know. But it's more than that ...whatever *"that"* is.

Last weekend was significant ...in many ways. I can't help but think about it ...can you? I know your head if full of questions I can't answer, if I could, they would be meaningless, (or either my questions) and hence, the infinite dilemma of whether the answers were yours or someone else's. I know enough not to go that road ;)) Questions of whether or not to do the "right thing" or listen to what your heart tells you to ...and those rare and beautiful eclipses where the two are indistinguishable... ooooh ...now I'm getting wet, ...must be the feminine side of me, or the dog licking my hand ;) At some point you'll get to a place where everything makes sense, and I'm going to be around. Enjoy the good moments and don't be in such a hurry to raze them from your memory just to make sure that the source of the experience, the "feeling" lies anywhere but within yourself. Wholeness is not a place, it is, I believe,

Newton's 4th law of "e"motion ...a physical impossibility, because what we are today, is not what we will be tomorrow... (Sorry, perhaps not what you wanted to hear) ...we are but human snowballs accumulating and growing as we roll along. We don't meet people who complete us, but if we are lucky, we meet people whom we are incomplete without, you are such a person for me. There are *Places* in our lives... places we pass by, ...places we stop and visit, ...places we feel safe, and places we call home. Perhaps the most we can hope for is a "place" where we are allowed to BE whole. The crux of the lesson is not to look for "wholeness," but to learn how to "be." To glance in the mirror and take stock of oneself, the good,... the bad,... the ugly... and still feel loved, understood... and accepted. I am such a place for you.

Don't be confused, I don't want to be the getaway car, I want to be the highway. Not the vehicle that will take you "there" as if "*there*" existed. We have many vehicles over the course of our lives, we exhaust them, grow tired of them, outgrow them ...they no longer meet our needs, but the highway is endless and ever-changing, challenging us, "smacking" our ass ;) ...and yet, ...rising up to meet us as well ;) You say I'm gentle, sweet, and I am ...with you at least. But don't make the mistake of casting me in one ...or even two roles Rae. I am those things and more, the blue-collar man/the white-collar man, the cerebral man/the fool, the poet/the comedian. I'm the patient impatient man, the rough looking bastard with a boyish grin, the insightful single dad, YOUR faithful infidel. I'm a REALLY nice guy ...who's the asshole that fucking another man's wife.

Want to know what I've seen down the road a ways, the path narrows, they always do, and we only get to take a few trusted, proven friends with us. Beyond that very liberating point where you learn to say "yes" to temptation comes an even more satisfying place where you can say "no," where you don't have to take advantage of every fucking opportunity because in the *wholeness* of that moment you recognize that you have all that you need inside yourself.

There's even a place beyond the question of "Can you be unfaithful to another, to be faithful to yourself?" where the real quagmire and paradox arises when being unfaithful to another is being unfaithful to yourself... how fucked up is that? But you and I, we can't be unfaithful to each other unless we betray that trust and honesty. We're beyond the introductory bullshit required classes. I know you've got curiosities that I can't satisfy. But I've proven my mettle where that's concerned ;)

I like this place of ours where we get together and our needs are mutually met... will you meet me there? Can you feel my warm breath on your neck, my hand on that pretty ass, my cheek to your cheek? I'm always with you, that part of me that only

belongs to you. I'll be out and about, let me hear from you if you wish. As usual, and always...

Love,

-Jake

He knew he wouldn't hear from her, but he had to write just the same. She had predictably fallen into a post-New Orleans funk and he needed her to hear something contrary to the voice in her head. His son was at a friend's house for the night. The *static* was visiting him like an aftershock from the previous weekend's earth shaking. He would call Nicole and they would get a bite to eat, and then return to his place. *"Nice tattoo"* she admired as he bared himself and they headed to bed, touching it gently as it was still healing. *"Thanks, it's been a long time in the making,"* is all he offered. Beyond that, she wouldn't ask about his weekend and he wouldn't volunteer any details, the nature of their arrangement didn't require it, and they picked up where they had left off, enjoying each other's company and growing closer, *or as close as they could...*

It was now late October, *"a beautiful time in North Carolina,"* which also coincided with his yearly physical and visit to Dr. "V." While no man above forty years of age looks forward to these occasions, he generally welcomed the annual opportunity for her to tell him how healthy he was. Everything was great, except for a lump on his prostate, a *nodule* she called it. It had been there the previous year and she had subsequently sent him to an Urologist, a man he couldn't forget because of the disheveled *mad scientist* look ...and the brown stains on his white jacket. Jake's blood-work was great, and he was of such a young age the specialist dismissed it as a 1% chance of being something of concern. This year however, "V" wasn't going to be as understanding, and like a mother, and the prudent professional that she was, she prescribed a biopsy for the man she was genuinely fond of to eliminate any doubts.

It was mid-November before the procedure took place. Rene, bless her heart, would accompany her son's father because he would need a driver afterward, and she would accompany him again the following week when he went to get the results. Take note that anytime your doctor won't give you the results over the phone, it's **not** a good sign. A **1mm** spot would accomplish what a half-dozen or so good men hadn't, and bring the man sober to his knees, or at least cause him to take a seat. *"You must have me confused with someone else,"* he blurted out as the word cancer echoed in the small room, there was some shock and disagreement in the minutes that followed and almost immediately things took on a pace and a sense of urgency beyond his control.

He'd had time to ponder the potential outcome since the possibility arose a year earlier, but the news and accompanying sensation was something he was unprepared for. He was momentarily dismantled. If coffee is a diuretic, the word *cancer* is a laxative, because he damn sure 'bout shit his self.

He had learned about the *teenage fallacy* in his developmental psych class, it was presented as an explanation for some teenage behavior. Because they are *teen*agers, adolescents naturally think they'll live to be old, a valid assumption, and one we don't want to deprive them of. But the problem arises in the accompanying misguided notion they can therefore afford to be reckless because their entire lives are ahead of them ...the *fallacy* being that youth in itself is a defense against death. As a **middle-aged teenager** he was now experiencing a modified version. While as adults we have witnessed mortality and have an active awareness of our own, our *fallacy* is that we'll live to that age of average life expectancy at least before dealing with it beyond that awareness. But the fallacy had abruptly succumbed to reality, as if the lifetime warranty had been violated because he hadn't rotated the tires or had some other necessary maintenance.

His child was the first concern that crossed his mind, but Rae would be the first person he thought to tell, and the **first** call he made from the parking lot. She had initially expressed a desire to go with him to the visit ...but he knew that to be unrealistic. It was obvious the news caught her off guard as well and he could hear the undeniable concern and sincerity in her initial, *honest* reaction ...then a disconnect of sorts, an uncomfortable pause and awkward silence as if the reality of what a prostate cancer diagnosis comes with was racing through her mind as well, and her concern, being evident as it was towards the man she *loved* and *cared* about, was not as great as her concern for herself and her *needs,* and that *"there ain't enough of me to go around"* tone in her unspoken words he had become painfully too familiar with, was inaudibly loud to the man who had guessed her password. It had to be deafening. Everyone he would tell afterward, was a matter of responsibility and personal business.

Rene had done more than her position as ex-wife demanded, so over the course of the next month he would drive himself to six different doctor appointments at area universities and nationally renowned Cancer Centers of Excellence. He had time to educate himself, and showed up at each one with a list of questions, statistical data, and other disease specific medical terminology and the questions he asked got ambiguous answers, and only gave rise to more questions.

The more he studied the subject, the more he realized there was an atmosphere of uncertainty, they were essentially offering treatment more out of fear of what they **didn't** know, than what they **did**. Make no mistake, the only time *Cancer* is ever mentioned in a positive sense is in the daily horoscope. The word is scary, but it represents over two hundred different diseases, and they are not all created equal. Prostate cancer is especially ambiguous since it is often slow growing and inane, ...more men die *with* it than *from* it. But he was unusually young, the average age of diagnosis sixty-eight, and he had a boy to raise and he wasn't ready to forfeit his spot on the planet either.

It presented quite a dilemma for the man. For every article in a medical journal that came out espousing one theory or hypothesis, there would inevitably be an opposing or contradicting one in another publication. It was akin to politics, the politics of the prostate, surgeons and radiologists the respective republicans and democrats so to speak, and let's not forget the independents ...the research community, and Jake's prostate appeared to be the bill before congress. Everyone was in agreement he had prostate cancer and that it needed to be treated, except of course him.

Chunk went with him to the first appointment, but only for support, if asked he would confess he was scared shitless, those settings are as intimidating and ominous as a courtroom, your fate is being determined, but Jake was extremely calm and prepared, and his friend taken aback as he put the expert in a corner on the issue, the numbers didn't add up, *autopsies of men who died of other causes suggested there was an X-minus-10 factor, or essentially 40% of 50 year-olds had some degree of the disease, 50% of 60 year-olds and so on and so on, it rose proportionately with each decade of life, for men his age it was suggested only 1 in 1000 cases were detected, and roughly 1 in 6 or approximately 18% of those "diagnosed" died from the disease,* and he had the least possible amount of the disease detectable.

As with any scientific data, the numbers were often subjective and *cooked,* and the abundance of information only added to the confusion and concern. He had seen three surgeons and three radiologists, and the last of the men, shut the door and told him he thought Jake to be right, and he was extremely knowledgeable, not a hack.

The absent-minded professor as Jake came to think of him, because he usually started their appointments by asking him how his wife and daughter were, knew his business, and he confirmed to Jake that in fact they were over-detecting and over-treating the disease, and that he would follow him if he chose to wait, and monitor him. Jake had not been seeking someone to tell him what he wanted to hear, but an honest perspective, and while the last thing the doctor would always say was that *"Ideally we'd like to remove it ...but I don't believe that'll be necessary just yet."* He had now found an ally in his battle.

From there on out it was as if he was Sherlock Holmes and the case of **The Eighteen-Per-Cent Solution**, or _dilemma_ as it were, set out to prove his prostate innocent ...the innocence project of Jake's prostate, before its proposed execution. Prostate cancer is the Rodney Dangerfield or Vanilla Ice of cancers ...considered curable, it doesn't get any respect. What's often not revealed in that discussion is how *curable* is defined in that sense ...*a ten-year disease free period* is considered cured, until that one molecule of cancer that slipped out the backdoor as the knife was being wielded or the laser irradiating the gland resurfaces, angry at the initial onslaught, its home in the gland now gone and thus relocated and colonized elsewhere, and it has typically brought friends with it ...more cancer. What is also less publicized about the statistics they promote for the high success rates is that they are very doctor dependent ...the average SAT score may be 1000, but not every student is making that grade, and likewise some doctors are more experienced and have better results than others and no one seemed to know their own individual statistics, or were prepared to share.

Lastly, and perhaps what was central to this for Jake was the fact there is also little said of the consequences that follow treatment, incontinence and impotence, and Jake was uncomfortable with the idea of stuff coming out of his penis when he didn't want it to, and nothing coming out of it when he did. You've heard the word *cock* a number of times, it's a sexual phrase, but in many respects prostate cancer is more about **pussy** and the fact there wouldn't be any in his future. Despite the propaganda, sex as he knew and enjoyed it was all but a memory after either treatment. Radiation or surgery ...it amounted to a sexual lobotomy, and if you've gathered anything about the man during the course of this tale, it's that he was a sexual being and he *loved* **pussy**, a lot of it, and if you remove that from the equation, *that* man would cease to exist.

And so he did the unthinkable, which was nothing, but it was well thought out, not out of denial but awareness, not because he was uninformed but because he was educated. That decision was not an easy decision to arrive at, to live with the knowledge that something inside of you is conspiring against you, but he appeared content with his choice. It's not a decision that's widely advocated, about 5% of cases, mostly elderly men who opt to go the "*Watchful Waiting,*" or "*Active Surveillance,*" route. But he had searched himself for the meaning between *living* and being *alive*, and he saw it as trading one kind of waiting for another, waiting for it to possibly progress and worsen vs. waiting for it to come back. Besides, it was his cancer, and if it were anything like him it would lack ambition and have a hard time finishing what it started.

He was essentially saying that it wasn't going to be a problem, but the knowledge it was there, and potentially meant to do him harm might be difficult for the Obsessive/Compulsive man, except it changed him instead. The *static* that had always lacked a purpose, a reason for its existence, found one in the cancer and in the process had strangely given it balance. But this is not a story about cancer, or those personal choices, only how it was a piece of the puzzle that both clouded the picture, and yet brought clarity to it as well.

At first there was a great need to tell others, but that *soon* passed. There's only one thing worse than telling people bad news and having them not care, and that's having them pretend to, and the cancer's appearance on the scene had been like a ***litmus test*** for friends. It had shown the true colors of some folks, some people ran towards him ...and some others ran the opposite direction as fast as they could. He hated to break it to Nicole, it seemed extremely heavy for the casualness of their relationship, but she was in that group of people that ran toward him, and she would be there waiting for him in the weeks to come.

She came to see him the weekend before Christmas, and for the man who felt his sexuality and masculinity threatened she would give herself to him in a most loving and reaffirming way, erasing all doubts to his value as a man, or her feelings for him. In the morning she awoke to find him staring at her as if studying her. *"What is it?"* She said, halfway embarrassed, halfway concerned. *"Nothing,"* he replied reassuringly, moving the hair from her face as if posing her, *"I'm just sketching a mental picture of you, now pretend to be sleeping so I can finish it."* If Rae was the woman he would have designed for himself, Nicole was the woman the people who knew him best would have designed and desired for their friend …and he couldn't help but notice the resemblance.

She didn't **know** about Rae, but she **knew** in that way women do. She had appreciated his honesty and respectfulness of her. What concerned her more was the path he seemed to be leaning towards with his health. It bothered her and she told him so, told him she would still be there, you won't find a kinder, more wonderful gift in the entirety of this tale.

For single adults with children, meeting the kids is like a teenager meeting the parents, except in reverse order, it's the last thing you do relationally. After the informal screening process that occurs, it's an indication of a relationship moving in a more serious direction when you invite someone into your child/children's lives, and Nicole did just that. It was Christmas, only a month after he had learned of his illness, they had been regularly involved for four months now. It was that point where grownups do those things, and the point at which he had historically bailed, become the *"asshole that didn't show up at the picnic with her friends, the Holiday dinner with the family, or who simply stopped calling,"* it was that inevitable moment of truth, and he didn't blink, but politely declined.

Her intuition told her that he probably would, but it was on a proverbial *check-down list* as she was heading towards a conclusion of her own. It wasn't as easy as it usually was for our man, but these were difficult times and while he wanted to be selfish and keep her in his life, that ace in the hole, he couldn't mislead her.

When all was said and done he **wanted** to see the woman he had grown close to and extremely fond of, but he **needed** to see the woman he loved. And he and Rae had made plans to get together the holiday weekend. It would be the first time since the diagnosis. It was the last time he'd see the woman he called "pebble."

She left sometime during the course of the next evening while he slept. He found a note the next morning, it would appear she had brought it with her. Unusual perhaps, but like the individual who had deservingly asked for a promotion, yet anticipated its courteous refusal she had come prepared to tender her *resignation.*

It read:

*I was optimistic for a time, there were some nice moments and the potential was there. You're good for a woman's ego you know, not a pretty boy but a beautiful man. I appreciated the honesty, it's rare these days. She's a lucky woman, I hope what you have with her is what you need it to be. My grandmother would say this to friends when they parted, so I say it to you now, **"May you go in a good way, and love and happiness follow."** Take care of yourself. Don't bother to call, we both know you were never really here ...even when you were.*

And the *rolling stone* gathers no *pebble*... She didn't sign it ...just a red lipstick kiss. Chunk wept when Jake eventually shared it with him, and a guy called "Chunk" don't weep. If he'd known at the time how things were going to unfold he probably would've tried to knock some sense into his friend, but he was in such a fragile state it might have ruined the boy, he was already *fractured*. She had brought peace to his life at a troubled time when he needed it, and he

317

would miss them both. To be sure, you could find the note alongside that yellow barrette …and his other amorous keepsakes.

As for the woman, he wouldn't know where to file her, "**N**" or "**P**" …and maybe he wasn't ready to. He didn't have the accompanying sense of relief this time, but began to tremble, an indication perhaps of the uncertainty in the decision he had made, or that had been made for him… As if the low fuel indicator on the dash had lit up telling him he had 15 miles left in the tank and he was 30 miles past the last station that boasted **"Last Gas For 60 Miles."** You do the math. We've all heard there's a difference between being alone and being lonely. It wasn't apparent *just* yet, but that difference is somewhere about here.

CHAPTER 15

WHEN THE DEVIL BEAT HIS WIFE

He told himself he was making the trip to Raleigh because he needed to get out, but it was Christmas ...where was there to go? Rae was supposed to have called earlier that day to let him know when to come by, they had communicated back and forth about it for weeks, but when she hadn't ...well, we've been there before ...and some mechanisms, some de-*vices* don't need much oiling and it could not have gotten any worse, until of course ...it did, ...when he saw the unfamiliar car in the driveway.

He became that guy, that guy that does the thing many of us would've thought about doing but wouldn't have the nerve. And he did so understanding the consequences, or maybe misunderstanding them as much as one can in that moment of temporary **sanity**. He stopped his truck in the middle of the street and paused for a moment, staring at the house he knew to be holding secrets like an oversized heart-shaped box, its lock now broken. He then proceeded to walk up another man's driveway to confront a wife about being with someone other than her husband, someone other than him. What *the* fuck?

If there's been any justice done to the telling of this tale, there's no need to try and explain what was going through the man's head at that moment, it would probably be easier to say what wasn't. They'd been intimate in ways few people ever are. In retrospect he had kept so many secrets, as much as anything he just needed her to know that he knew who she really was, and that he had for some time.

He studied the car, a Porsche 914, candy-apple red, nicely restored and in typical fashion he committed the plate to memory. He paused to look in the carport window. He could see them in the dimly lit kitchen, barely a breath's distance between them. He had been there in that moment with her, had been that guy, he knew what she intended to happen. It was her *play* and he knew how it ended.

Who knows if a heart makes a sound when it breaks, but he could tell you. His eyes became moist at the sight …and then he had that "**thought**," that *thought* which was "<u>unthinkable</u>," that thought he hadn't allowed himself to "think" because it meant that in that month's time he had been driving *himself* to doctor appointments and making decisions about his health, *quality* of life, of *life* and *death* …of her and Nicole, that she'd been thinking about the diagnosis as well and *perhaps* come to the decision that if he wound up not having any value to her as a sexual partner, then he had no value to her as a man, as a friend, and she was already *interviewing* his replacement or had hired a "temp." It wasn't just that he might *need* her …it was that she <u>wouldn't</u> *need* him if he couldn't help her with her "needs." It was "unthinkable" in that way a parent won't allow themselves to think of their child dying, as if simply thinking about it might somehow superstitiously make it come true, because if it were *more* than a thought the <u>reality</u> would be unbearable and unspeakably "cruel," …like Merriam-Webster *cruel.* And somewhere deep inside the man that lonely, ostracized and once unattractive child felt an overwhelming anger and familiar pain. He **couldn't** have been that wrong about her. Only weeks before they had shared *another* loving and unforgettable experience …and he had the *ink* to prove it.

So he stepped to her door, that *boundary* he had crossed thirteen months prior, only now he had the attitude and appearance of a man intruded *upon* and **not** the intruder. He then began to pound the door as if it somehow represented Timothy, Tony and the half dozen other men she'd slept with …*aside* from her husband since their involvement began, knowing there would be a swell of anxiety inside by doing so. Rae answered it surprised and alarmed at first to find Jake uninvited, looking prodigious and surly like that *mangled dog* come in the yard. He's a sizable man and the fella inside looked understandably concerned, but he wasn't the object of his ire, she was. He was swollen with emotions, sober yet inebriated by a dangerous cocktail of anger, betrayal, and immense disappointment and hurt. Inflamed …and at the heart of it all was the friendship, fidelity among the unfaithful, about the "love" that existed between them ...*or the apparent absence of it* …but he wouldn't get past her.

There are two times when a dog is truly dangerous, when it's hurt and when it's scared and he was both. But however imposing he may have been, if there's one thing unanimously and undisputedly more dangerous in nature than that rogue male it's the mother looking to protect her pups, her cubs or whatever the fucking analogy you choose, and he was not going to present a threat to that. She might have cared less about Glen as a man in that moment, but Glen represented the stability of her kids' present and future well-being, and she wasn't going to jeopardize that for Jake. She loved her children, beyond that everyone else was conditional and a matter of convenience. It was such an intense confrontation that he wouldn't really remember all he had said, but he would never forget what she had as she minced no words and delivered her message very clearly, all with a scornful yet trademark *southern twang. "Don't tell me what you've done for me, after all I've let you do to me. I didn't ask anything of you. My advice to you is not to do anything you don't want to do in the future. Now get off my property, I never want to see you again,"* and then she stood there to make certain he left, the fella inside peering around a corner, in his own state of "shock and awe," and he looked a lot like that guy Vincent.

Jake briefly pondered busting in and making a mess, in light of recent events it would not have been surprising. He hadn't been thinking clearly, and it was unplanned ...but it's doubtful it went as he had *thought* or *planned*. He had hoped she would apologize, cry ...lie, or something that would make him feel justified, an attempt at making him feel better, but instead he only felt dissatisfied at the outcome and even more hurt if possible. In hopes and need of a gentle kiss and a lover's warm embrace that evening, he had instead gotten a tongue-lashing and verbal bitch slap, as if the stud horse he had been was gelded on her front porch.

Sometimes a minute is painfully brief, like the minute after the last call "Now Boarding" as you say goodbye to a loved one at the terminal, or painfully long, like the minute holding your breath underwater, but in the end, both are just sixty seconds ...just a minute. And this would simply be one of the most painful of his life ...the anguish written all over his face, the indifference on hers, all with a few harsh words, however deservedly spoken. And just like that *utility* became *futility*, "*a part*" became "*apart*." They say there's inevitably a straw that breaks every camel's back, but it wouldn't be the number of men in this case as you might suspect, but the woman unaided in the long run who would bring him figuratively to his knees.

There's no understating their intimacy and involvement, she was the woman in his life ...he her lover, confidante, and *stalker*. He knew her secrets and had kept them, especially the ones she *hadn't* shared with him. Love is a primal emotion, the earliest beings knew the feeling of love ...they "*felt*" it, the word served as an acknowledgement of it, but it would complicate their situation. Every time it was written at the end of an email or spoken at the end of a phone call, in the throes of passion or at the announcement of a cancer diagnosis, it brought with it implications of concern for one another, expectations of caring, an intimate contract. At its very least, reduced to its molecular level, an indication of friendship, it wasn't afforded a casual reference. He had that for her, it was evident, even if *evidenced* in some very disturbing behavior and obsession, but he had also felt it from her, he trusted his assessment of that, it wasn't merely wishful thinking. She had offered the words and sentiment willingly of her own volition ...but if *affirmation* is a statement of truth, and *confirmation* proof of it, her love was **un**confirmed as her actions were continually at odds with the connotations the word demanded.

He knew she had other allegiances, stronger alliances and commitments, and there are two sides to every coin and Jake would not deny where he fell in the great scheme of things, he had always known as the person outside the marriage he was dispensable, but the timing was unforgiving and so was he. He couldn't cast any stones, he wasn't without guilt or sin, but like some romantic hit-and-run he was wounded and she knew it. It wasn't as if she *couldn't* be there for him in some limited capacity, she'd simply *chosen* not to be, had simply chosen not to offer any comfort ...*again*, and he was having some extreme difficulty with the accumulation of similar events.

He went through something akin to the five stages of grief on the way home ...at least twice, Denial, Anger, Bargaining, Depression, **un**-Acceptance, rinse and repeat. He hadn't cried like this when his mother died, hadn't wept at the announcement of his wife wanting a divorce. The death of a loved one, the death of a love were mournful but could be buried. How could he put to rest something that never really existed? The profundity of that awareness at a moment of such great need for compassion, compounded by all the collateral issues of anger, illness, insecurity, and ...*fear*, made it exponentially worse, and it damaged him. If you had possessed some *psychological* 3-D glasses the man would have resembled a fragile emotional mosaic ...his life in pieces, yet invisible to anyone, and the love and responsibility to his son the <u>only</u> thing holding it all together.

But ...it was unacceptable. And in the days that followed, like the boyfriend who realizes he has left his favorite shirt at his ex's after the breakup, or the young man who had given an heirloom engagement ring to a girl and not gotten it back after they called the wedding off... Rae had something that belonged to him, and he intended to get it back. Inadvertently honest, he had shown her his underbelly, he wanted his relationship with her to be the one where it was safe to be vulnerable, to be afraid, to be human, but she had demonstrated her aversion to his drama, and graphically displayed her ability to disappoint. She only had room in her life for relationships that had benefit to her, it had always been about Rae you'll remember. But the view from the inside looking out is very different than the view outside looking in, and each of their perspectives was naturally skewed as a result.

He was well beyond the point where sex was the only commonality between them. He'd missed that exit entirely, or to be honest, willfully ignored it. What he had wanted more than anything was some semblance of affection and *verification* that he was more than just the unpaid hired help, but in a painful analogous vein, they say people don't pay for sex, they pay to leave afterward, and that all too familiar, and now hypocritical realization that ***friends-with-benefits*** was a misnomer, there was no benefit without the friendship, disagreed with him on numerous levels. If he could balance that equation he could walk away and call it even, but she was noncompliant. And he had the tenacity of a *back creek* turtle, or "*cooter*" as they were called, which the local lore said would hold onto something until it thundered, and he had latched onto her and was holding on to his place in her life whether she liked it or not, …hanging by that worn out *thread*. It was about as productive as trying to milk a bull, but he was nothing if not persistent.

Like a tire that begins to wobble when it's out of balance, he had lost his center of gravity, that ability to trust his gut that had been key to his survival, thinking unclearly and dangerously close to losing his shit. If someone asked him how he was doing, he would reply with the habitually "great" automated response, but it was a bit like asking a man how his roof was holding up to which he replies "Its fine, except when it rains."

There's a scene in the movie **Pulp Fiction** where Bruce Willis' character Butch asks Marsellus, (Ving Rhames) "You okay?" after he's been ass-raped by a redneck, to which he replies, "**Naw man, I'm pretty fuckin' far from okay.**" ...Jacob Arnett was a long way from being "great," his heart not only broken and scattered, but parts missing, and he would not be whole for a time to come ...an emotional Humpty Dumpty. For a man who was no stranger to unfriendly moments, it would stand as the unfriendliest of all. He thought himself to be immune to it, vaccinated so to speak, but he wasn't. The self-imposed romantic solitary confinement that had defined most of his adult life only revealed to be what he thought a "safe distance," his aversion to hurting others, in reality a fear of being hurt. The pride he had taken in his self-reliance, his ability to get by without needing anyone but the boy ...what he had perceived as strength now exposed as weakness. The child who had grown up with much love to give, became a man who loved deeply, and conversely hurt deeply as well and he wished for a pain that he was used to.

There were now blind spots in his confidence and shadows on his psyche. She had knocked loose the keystone of his being, and the ground underneath his life left unstable. It was a difficult time for the man, he missed some people he had lost ...and some he had *given* away.

The emotions would exhaust and consume him, until like the influenza, he had sweated them out, and once he had it became something all together different for the man. Like the romantic squatter that he discovered himself to be, he had imagined it like some *adverse possession* that if he hung around long enough without being evicted he could eventually lay claim to some permanent part of her landscape by default. He should've had a bag of essential emotions packed though, ready to go at a moment's notice, but he hadn't seen it coming. In that **minute** she had stolen a **lifetime's** worth of hard earned instinct and intuition, the utilities that had kept the man alive. See, "Sometimes gettin' what you want ain't a good thing"...be careful what you wish for. He hated himself for being such a fool, but he found it necessary to continue to be her secret-keeper and wouldn't tell anyone. His illicit association to a married woman wouldn't find a sympathetic audience anyway, so he subsequently sequestered and quarantined it from the other aspects of his life. Life waits for none of us and important decisions still had to be made and he was wishing he had a mulligan of the love variety right about now, an emotional do-over. It was as if the sky had darkened with arrows all pointed at him. Poor fella....

None of us is more than the *wrong* heartache or the *right* misfortune and tragedy from coming off the rails, and anyone of these things singularly might have been enough. It was as if he had one foot on the platform and the other on a train waiting to pull out of the station, that being his feelings towards Rae. As a consequence he couldn't be all in with Nicole, and as time would tell, she wasn't one to wait. At a most inopportune time Rae had vacated the premises *...or asked him too*, and he found himself alone with both feet on the platform as Nicole and those possibilities had already exited the station in the opposite direction. He had invested in something that had no future, and not invested in something that had. It was the concurrence of two opposing forces, like *loving* someone and *hating* them in the same moment, *finding* what you seek yet getting *lost* in the discovery, like *rain* on a *sunny day* ...when the *devil beat his wife*.

It felt as though his life was being drawn and quartered, and the bittersweet ambiguity of what was happening tugged at him like a riptide. You'd think that indignity, that inhumane and gross insensitivity of the moment would have been enough for him to wash his hands of her, but you'll remember the boy had gotten his ass whooped in a weakened state before, and he knew he would get up. If he had to walk her down to square things, then that's what he was gonna do. The reality of what had just happened wouldn't enable this man to move forward, so instead he would tell himself he understood her fear, the innocent considerations that lay within the confines of her life, and how it didn't provide for disruptive emotional entanglements ...she had all she could handle, and it was he who lost sight of the boundaries, erased and redrawn them, and in so doing trespassed on her precious properties. Maybe she did care, maybe she always had, but there was too much weighing in the balance. The gravity of which outweighed his needs. His forgiveness however would not be altruistic in nature, only a necessary lie he had to tell himself. He wanted to get back to being the man that he was, but something inside his peculiar makeup wouldn't allow him to leave without collecting what he had lost, what she had taken from him.

At some point, you had to feel sorry and concerned for the girl. In a sense Glen had picked the ripest peach and chosen not to eat it, or maybe to be more accurate, it had fallen in his lap, and he had chosen not to eat it. Regardless, he was letting it go to waste, and there's not much distance between ripe and growing rotten. And Jake had become like a feral dog ...check that, a *rabid* feral dog. She had offered the man a very nice arrangement conducive to his lifestyle and inclinations. She told him the parameters and he agreed to them, but the rules had not really been enforced ...and not enforced, they might just as well not existed.

Something beautiful and unique had happened unexpectedly to them both in the beginning, and it had bloomed *magnificently* several times, but she was able to let go of it, and he wasn't. Truth be told, if she'd been readily available like all the other women that passed through his life, he probably would have had that same awkwardness in the morning in asking her to leave, and it would have lasted as long as that *carton of milk*, but she wasn't. She began to feel as though she had picked up some *psycho-sexual* hitchhiker, and couldn't very well call 911 or ask for help, cornered, instead of slamming the door in his face, she had flung it wide open so that he could get a good look at the reality of their situation.

Two roads had diverged in a yellow wood, and he could not travel both ...and be the one traveler, and so he took the one his heart demanded of him that turned out to be a dead-end, and would've done so again, it would have been uncharacteristic of him not to. Was it worth the pain *"that it might inflict?"* Only he could answer that. He may have been some other folks' best friend ...but he was his own worst enemy, and that was never meant to be anything other than a sad, heartrending truth.

CHAPTER 16

MEANINGFUL COINCIDENCE

In the end it seems she didn't really have a plurality of faces, she just had the one, and underneath the surface it wasn't really pretty, just coldhearted, with a lack of originality surrounding the same sad, overdone story. He came to see her as not really having the range of characters in her repertoire he had first thought, not as if she played a number of drastically different roles, she just placed herself in different scenes and settings with an assortment of co-stars. Like a piece of driftwood, carefully arranged on a coffee table it can be a decorative centerpiece, placed in the yard it was just a stick, in the fireplace a log, or left alone on a beach ...simply what it was all along, just another piece of unremarkable driftwood.

She didn't have that much variety about her, only adeptness and skill at the presentation, all of which hinged upon an unfamiliar and first-time audience because it didn't have the depth or mystery that merited an encore, except unfortunately for him. Despite the fact it was a one-act play, it was still an enjoyable show, and during the course of its run he had been the villain, the hero, the audience and critic. But no longer that same man she had invited into her life. He'd suffered that moment when he saw himself in the mirror and caught the reflection of *jealousy, deception, vengeance, and ...obsession ...**not very attractive either***. Not the image of the man whom he wanted to be seen as, or the man he once thought himself to be. She'd never meet anyone quite like him again and it'd be wrong not to at least suggest there's a measure of loss and degree of sadness for her in that statement. In spite of everything **you** now know, the woman had never felt unloved by the man ...even under some *strenuous* circumstances.

As mentioned some time ago, peaks and valleys, extensive plateaus and piedmonts, had characterized his sexual life and so too their relationship. That was part of the allure, and the infrequency fueled the desire and wouldn't allow him to get his fill, never satiated, and thus always hungry for time with her. That inability to get bored with each other had helped it endure, he hadn't been saddled with the responsibilities of a typical relationship, only the strangely complex complications of the arrangement that were somehow attractive to the strangely complex and complicated man, even his uncomfortable awareness of her behavior and tendencies that should have turned him off, turned on his competitive nature. Like the image his tattoo presented, unrestrained the relationship would have devoured itself and expired in the process. It could not have survived at such a high altitude of emotion before suffocating, burned up with the expediency of a tissue in a furnace and been in the books or his *library* so to speak, and he already "moved on" like all similar liaisons in his past.

In the end it was not how she did or did not feel about him that he missed or was of importance, but how he felt about her ...and how she made him feel about himself. That was among the things he lost that night. It's hard to understand, but like he would say *"Don't tell me you know where I'm coming from unless you've been where I've been."*

He loved her, so much so he would even come to concede to understanding why she had done what she did. In all fairness to them *both*, she loved him too, but she did what was instinctual. She cared ...to a degree, to the extent she was capable, that her situation would allow, like a sad story on the evening news, until another would come along. She was mired in her own sorrow, she couldn't help him with his. She told herself it was the kindest thing she could do, but as far as he was concerned there were a lot of ways she could have cut that cake and this was the most *unkindest* cut of all...

It would be painstakingly arduous, the long game is, but like mud on your shoes, if you try to wipe it off while it's still wet it just makes a bigger mess. Instead he needed to give it time to "dry" before making any gestures. And with that in mind, the ending would begin, just as the beginning had begun, with words carefully chosen.

There is probably no combination of meaningful words in the English language that haven't been used together, but the assignment of meaning and the way they are heard can be greatly affected by the arrangement and timing of usage. Like the CD's he would burn, he knew that he could take the same twelve songs and order them differently and it would have a dramatic effect on the interpretation, and someone's appreciation for them. He was angry and intimately destroyed in a way only she could have done so ...and only she could repair. She was just angry, what he said next had to be perfectly arranged. The situation was as delicate as Middle East peace talks, she had his *mojo*, and he couldn't bring a verbal or emotional nuke to the negotiation, or there would be no further discussion.

So he unnaturally tempered his communications, aware that she was analyzing his words for evidence of anything remotely resembling "needy" and things once said could not be unspoken where she was concerned. With that understanding, the landscaper surveyed the situation and approached it like an essay assignment, "In 500 words or less, defuse this woman's anger and concerns, express yours in a non-threatening way, lay the groundwork for achieving your goal without revealing what that is." It would need to be honest, to the point, shallow, and yet so deep she could fall in it and not get out.

He needed to give her just the tip of that literary 12-incher and make her want for the rest. This is what he presented:

I'm sorry but I can't apologize, to do so would lack sincerity and diminish the words, and I reserve them for necessary occasions. I have to ask though, what was it that hurt so much when you busted in that hotel room and found Frank with another woman? Were those feelings relegated to the fact you were married, or that he broke your heart? That's intentionally rhetorical of course, we both know the answer, but I'd like to hear you explain how that's any different than what I'm feeling and the way that I reacted. I told you once that if "the time should come when the thought of NOT having me in your life as a friend/lover produced a greater sense of relief, than of sadness," I'd be gone, all you had to do was say so ...but you didn't.

I suspect on some level you must wish your husband cared as much. If I'm sorry for anything it's that I miss the way I've felt about you, you've made me want to be a better man and not demanded it of me. I really wanted to write and tell you how bad you hurt me, but I kept defaulting to the realization that I let myself get hurt by you instead. That was a jagged pill to swallow to say the least, but I needed to take my medicine where it was concerned. If you take the emotion out of our equation it's really rather pedestrian, and we both know it's been anything but ordinary. We've delighted in the fact that it existed, ...even if only in capsules and on the edge of our lives. Knowing it was there has given us both comfort, and unrest.

The good news is I still have feelings where you're concerned, just not the feelings you're accustomed to ...I couldn't resist ;) You deserve a good spanking... Keep an open mind will you, good/bad, yin/yang, love and hate ...sometimes the difference can be as indiscernible as the difference between *"something you'll always remember,"* and *"something you can't forget"* ...however slight the distinction, the distinction remains, that point where the two meet, where the one becomes the other. We're in that crevice, the gray area now. You're scratching your head I suppose ...or maybe not.

I know you don't want to hear it, but it needs to be said just the same ...we have unfinished business. The thoughts that are arcing through our heads and hearts right now, like the loose ends of a downed power-line, need to be tied up and dealt with. You mentioned you never wanted to see me again, but *Never* and *Always* are big words and you're going to find yourself missing me, and I'm not lost. I'm of the opinion we can still be of some value to one another on this journey. We have some hard-earned familiarity that would be a shameful waste and angry sex can be very gratifying, or so I recall... You'll hear from

me at some point in the not too distant future …if I don't hear from you, I'll assume you're okay with that.

-Jacob

He signed it with his given name, it was the first time he had done so. Like Raen, it was that name which only family and chosen family called him by, and there was an insinuation buried in the usage. Like that high-pitch whistle only a dog can hear, if she was keen enough to pick up on it, he wouldn't hear from her. And that would be a good thing. He needed to score a run here, but to get to home-plate you have to touch all the bases. Things were extremely fragile right now. It would be ill-advised to try and knock it out of the park right off the bat, just get to first base and go from there.

He had an agenda you'll recall, but he couldn't just ask for his dignity back …that would have been demeaning, and unsuccessful. So a second dialogue would begin, not one between two strangers who were curious about each other and exploring whether or not to act on that curiosity, but one between two people who knew each other all too well, and deciding whether or not that knowledge had a value greater than the attack against it, whether or not to maintain contact ...or so it had to seem. You have to build trust, you can't manufacture it, theirs had been broken and it would take a considerable amount of time to repair. He wouldn't wait anxiously this time to see if she responded, he knew that she wouldn't, because he knew her.

She was relieved to get the email, she had been concerned about where his head was at, and preoccupied about what he might do next. Son-of-a-bitch had come to her house like he owned it. Besides, he was right, she would come to miss him. She needed him to remind her how special she was in case others didn't take notice. So she took the bullets out of the metaphorical gun, and waited to hear from him. He would take his damn time in doing so.

Start to finish it would take fourteen months, fourteen months of listening to her complain, of telling her what she wanted to hear from him, pretending to be her cheerleader, her therapist, pretending to understand and be concerned, sympathetic. He had played many roles in his life, pretended to be many things ...among the most requested of them pretending to be "interested." And he did, and he did so very well. He should have been something other than he was. He would need to make her want to summon him, just as Cleopatra had pulled the asp to her own breast.

There wasn't a lot of sex the coming year, as if the cancer was an affliction he didn't want to expose anyone else to, obviously itself not contagious, but the tension and anxiety it brought potentially so. He was prepared to endure that himself, but not willing or able to *infect* someone else with it. It would've been unfair to burden another with that heaviness and he had enough to worry about in terms of how it might affect him, much less someone else ...and then there was the small matter of potential for disappointment, and he'd had enough of that. So the women he did encounter, he made no mention of it, he wouldn't see them again anyway, nor was it a topic available for discussion with Rae, she had forfeited that *security clearance*, and seemed unaffected by the loss.

It must've been difficult to have such strong feelings, but be inhibited, be incapable of being truly honest with someone you had been so intimate with, as if honesty was appreciated ...to a point, but it always had to be flattering, even when flattery was the furthest thing from his mind he would find something to say, even if it was just to echo what she was voicing. Jake would willingly confess that it was the kind of honesty akin to enabling, but the alternative was that there **was** no alternative. She had booby-trapped the relationship, and set up all kinds of metaphoric warnings, trip wires, to alert herself to any unhealthy attachment not to her liking, any potential threat, but the truth was he was not that nimble a man and each time he got close to what he sought, she withdrew.

It would not be an easy year for *the married girl* either though. He had scared her, and in doing so reminded her of all that she had to lose and how those she cared most about could get hurt in her selfish pursuits. But that itch wouldn't go away, and it wouldn't scratch itself. In a sense he had forced her *further* underground, reduced to anonymous one-night stands and while that can be a bumpy road for a single gal, it is much more so for a middle-aged married woman with three school-age children. The ability to screen her playmates and control the environment lost. He had long since closed the peephole into her activities, now unable and uninterested in protecting her, relying only on his knowledge of the woman, her behavior ...and his imagination, for what she might be doing extramarital-wise and how he could adapt to get in the game.

He shared his philosophy on life with Chunk once while tailgating one afternoon ...or at least his perspective on that day. He was of the opinion that the universe was comprised of dichotomies, opposites as it were. There could be no "light" without "dark," no "joy" without "pain," no "Yes" without "No," and infinite shades of compromise existed in between. That Good and Evil, Heaven and Hell exist within each of us, and there's an endless subliminal crusade going on to see which will prevail, a constant tug-of-war and balancing of the two. You remove one or diminish its presence, well it's true what they say, nature does abhor a vacuum, the other fills the void and the scales tip.

For a time they had been like a lock and key, she the place where he fit, where his heart felt at home; he the key that too perfectly filled a "loving" void in her life, but she had exiled him, and in the emptiness his departure had left, in the darkness of the underground she'd been forced deeper in to, perversion and deviancy flooded the space he had occupied. She'd had more intimacy with Jake than her husband since they'd met, more orgasms by the man than all others combined, important only in the level of comfort and trust it required. She had come to think of herself as the prize, he had done that for her, given her that *gift* at a time she felt inconspicuous, and she had been that rare love interest in his life, that top-shelf in his *library*.

Perhaps it had happened by accident, but it was of her design. Of course she would miss the man, she just couldn't admit it ...doing so would have resembled remorse and she couldn't shoulder that on top of everything else. So she pushed in the other direction, as people in denial are apt. But deviancy and perversion are not entirely the property or province of deviants and perverts. Just as we all have the physiological potential for addiction, we similarly have psychological proclivities for a departure from the norm, and she had been deprived of exploring hers. Sexual appetites, much like our appetites for food, evolve as we grow older. When we are young our taste-buds are incredibly sensitive, our appetite easily satisfied and our menu small, simple, bland and predictable, but as we age, those *taste-buds* dull, and we hunger for things not always on the menu, things we once thought unpalatable. Just as when we are young, the slightest of things *excite* us, as we grow older, _some_ people require more stimulation to arouse, and more importantly, satiate that instinctual craving and appetite, and *variety is the spice of life*. The girl had an unmistakable *kink* to her no doubt.

Her opportunities had always been limited, but with Glen's mother now living with them the cage that was her life had grown smaller. Like a driver at a red light who has waited for what seems like an eternity for it to change, and grown weary of waiting decides to run it, she would have to make her own opportunities, and unknown to Jake, taking incredible risks, exploring her limits and pushing the envelope. The establishments she found herself in not unsavory, but the patrons less appreciative and while she was often a trophy, she was never the prize.

Perhaps the Preacher's daughter had wanted to be punished, not because the "good" girl had been "bad," had been disloyal to a man she didn't love and should have divorced. She had done wrong to be sure, but been no more "good" or "bad" than Jake had. But she had turned her back to the most loving man in her life at a time when he needed some particular kindness, and she the sole possessor of it, knowing full well he would have stolen it for her if the circumstances were reversed. He had silently pardoned her for that, but the truth of the matter is, there are those sins others can forgive us for, which we can't forgive ourselves. And so we continue, as this was never a typical man/woman love story, but a love story nonetheless, and in the love, the betrayal, the pain, ...boo-coo sex, at the end of the day, in its essence ...a very human story.

Still insanely in tune with her, on an accurately forecasted unromantic Valentine's Day, like an assassin who had lain in wait for months disguised as Cupid, he sent her a pointed text, and in a moment of weakness, or want, she would steal away and call. He had succeeded in worming his way back into her life, into her confidence, that endearing fuck of a man. Not in the name of love so much as some sign that he had not been entirely wrong in his assessment of her feelings for him, to retake the trust in his instincts and intuition, and the accompanying self-respect he had **shat** on her porch. The dawg had succeeded in treeing the cat.

No longer a rescue mission, but salvage and recovery. And though he'd insinuated that it was no longer about the sex, that's a half-truth, it was about all of the things you know and imagine, but the sex was the manifestation of their feelings, the stage where it was acted out. It was and always had been first and foremost, a sexual relationship that had bled into other areas. The year they were involved had been a good year for the man, there had been much sex, but he'd only *made* love with the one woman. And he couldn't move on without picking up some necessities he had left behind.

When he met her it was as if his heart had eclipsed his mind, the two were in agreement for the first time in years, if not ever. But that moment on her doorstep, another eclipse had occurred, only this time his head eclipsed his heart, and the emotion that had colored the affair would fade into stark realization. She looked the same but he now saw her very differently, no longer full of vitality and sensuality, but sadness and exhaustion, still beautiful but unattractive, her sultry simply reduced to imperfection. They would meet at the place where it had all begun, Leon's.

He searched his inventory for the appetite he'd once had for her and it wasn't there, the desire and adoration gone, replaced with that **redrum**/\murder moment of seeing the true reflection in the mirror, and that what he thought he had seen didn't exist. Had it always been his projection of her significance in his life, and his perception of significance in hers? Probably not, but if we're *attracted to people who see us as we **want** to be* *seen, as we see ourselves,* then perhaps conversely by some sad irony and awareness, not so much to the people who've come to see us for who *we* really are… And they'd **both** lost their appeal.

We are an imperfect species. It is said people like us for our perfections and love us for our flaws. If you find someone who loves you in spite of them, it's a testament to its strength and legitimacy, and by that measure accurate to say that he loved her and always would, but he had come not to like her in the learning process. He wished it to be different, he wanted it to be, *but the heart has its reasons...*

She was no longer that quintessential M.I.L.F. he remembered her to be, but instead a W.I.F.E., a Woman I've Fucked Every-which-way, or just a wife... And someone else's at that, a fact that no longer sat well with him. The expiration date of it felt familiar. Perhaps she had felt it as well, and this was her way of giving him back what she had taken, her way of letting him let go of her. Who knows? For a time he wished he'd never met her, but only for a time. He'd loved her in a way he'd forgotten how, and nothing worth having comes without a price. It's impossible to be that intimate with another human and not leave part of yourself behind. They had conducted business of the most personal variety, made "intimate" transactions, trafficked in emotions, exchanged deeds to parcels of each other's emotional, spiritual, and sexual properties. She had made quite an impression on the man …and he would *long* feel the bruise. It's always the scars unseen that hurt the most.

Now that the moment was finally at hand, it was surreal, like an inmate serving a life-sentence who finds himself outside the prison walls at long last. The plan that had been the underlying theme of his life for over a year, the revenge-like element that had given his emotional OCD a bone to gnaw on, had worked. Now what? He had imagined it a hundred different ways. Fantasized he'd whip that shit until his *bone* collapsed, then paint a sticky portrait on her face... But he'd already rendered that masterpiece when she'd volunteered the canvas, and like a "*Smiley Face*" it could only have the one *interpretation* for him, reminiscent of a happier *period*.

Instead, what he wanted to do, what he **needed** to do was get to that moment and then as she lay begging for his attention and naked in *every* sense of the word, tell her he couldn't do it. Tell her that he wasn't attracted to her anymore, get dressed and leave her lying there in a lonely hotel room after he had spent months weakening her defenses, regaining her trust, and forcing her into an uncomfortable acknowledgement that she cared about him and loved him as well. That would be the closest he could come to what she had done to him, an act of cruelty only **he** could bestow upon her.

It would have killed her in a sense, or at least left her lifeless, taken that last bastion of *confirmed* desire and affection from her that she had privately clung to in her darkest moments during their year apart. He had worked so hard to get there and it had taken so long, when all was said and done he couldn't deny himself the satisfaction of getting a nut ...nor be as unkind. His goal and agenda had always been to get something of *his* back, not take something of *hers* in return. No matter how it had fueled the pursuit, even in the fantasy, he couldn't do it.   Love will take a bullet for you, hate will throw one at you, and he couldn't pull that trigger. I guess that says it all.

The occasion itself wasn't particularly memorable. It had too much baggage and associated expectation for it to have been, but like a psychological bloodletting, it was cathartic and it would give him the closure he sought, in that "*you can't move forward until you let go of the past*," way. A sad but necessary formality, like signing divorce papers …absent the marriage.   It would allow him to unburden himself, and perhaps for the first time in his life, say "***tag, you're it.***" The *dawg* had his day.

Whether you wish to call it "destiny," "fate," or mere "chance," the truth is that at the end of our days, perhaps some of the most significant occurrences, moments, and relationships in our lives are nothing more than just a matter of timing, a consequence of being in a certain place at a certain time …synchronicity, as it were, or "meaningful coincidence" as the case may be, whatever it was, it was indelible. Not a watermark, not a stain, but a *tattoo* on his heart.

In that collection of phrases he kept he had one that he had reserved for her, *"Some people come into our lives for a reason, some for a season, some for a lifetime ...and some for a day,"* and she was all of the above.

Let's face it, affairs are messy, they never end well. We make decisions in life that we have to live with, and he had no regrets only a bit of rumination, not a change of heart, but *a change of needs*. She would remain his favorite mistake, in the best "worst" year of his life, the third woman he would always love. But he wouldn't need to see her again, as if he had gotten that last necessary credit required for his *graduation*.

Amidst all the things he had felt was the desire to love again ...*unrestrained* and uncomplicated. She had planted that *seed* in him and it'd taken root. He knew that some of the most interesting and beautiful items in the landscape bloom late, and it was that season in his life. And in the continuing education of the man, she had given him a remedial course in what it would feel like when he found it. That was her *gift* to him.

He would write a last letter afterwards, it was an epilogue to their play, or perhaps an epitaph to the relationship, who knows for certain? He had never actually said goodbye to a woman.

It read:

Rae Anne,

Thanks for the opportunity to spend some *quality* time with you. It was "warm and pleasing," but I'll always miss the "*hot and bothered*." I am glad that I have served to make you feel better about yourself, but I must confess over the course of time I have come away from seeing you, or "not" seeing you as the case has often been, not feeling so positive about myself, beginning to realize the role I have been relegated to is one for which I am unsuited.

I am a different person for having known you, and I'm convinced overall that is a good thing. This "friendship" has however reached a point for me where it no longer

serves a purpose, and you told me once "I shouldn't do anything I don't want to" and this is that intersection where I must take a different path. While it has been sparse in terms of the time we have actually seen each other, I want you to know you have occupied much of my thoughts since that moment we first met.

I told you that "always" and "never" are big words, and I use them with caution, but I can say with some certainty that I will always love you, and I will never forget our moments together, only time will tell how we truly remember each other. Perhaps, if it is meant to be, we will see each other somewhere down the road. Life isn't linear, but cyclical ...rolling along, and sometimes we find ourselves in a familiar place with a familiar face.

I hope your journey takes you someplace agreeable. I am exiting stage left as they say ...Bogie and Bacall we're not ...but we will always have New Orleans ...and a couple of tattoos ;) Travel well...

Love,

-Jake

But he couldn't send it, no real surprise there "right?" It would just sit in his "**mail waiting to be sent**" folder indefinitely, *evidence* of his weakness where she would always be concerned ...the poor bastard. Apparently "goodbye" was another word he used with caution.

Instead he would simply put her where she rightfully belonged, "**R**" for Rae Anne, and he wouldn't think of her for a time, not like he had anyway. That was of course until he heard her name mentioned on the local evening News a couple of months later. The station's onetime weathergirl with the aptly exploited childhood nickname, the revered Preacher's daughter, the respected Professor's wife, the beloved Sportscaster's ex-wife, mother of three ...who just happened to be the woman he had secretly had a two year relationship with, was part of the broadcast again …only this time as a ***story***. Believe me when I tell you *everyone* was talking about it …except for our boy Jake. The quietly confident man was just concerned and quiet, and you and I know he had reason to be. The affair that had begun with the brilliance and perfection of a diamond had turned into a romantic kidney stone …and he had *passed* it, but it was far from <u>*behind*</u> him. Some secrets are indeed, begging to be told, silently screaming in need of a voice, seeking permission, clemency, or immunity from what they may reveal about us.

He had protected her in that regard you'll remember, but doing so had left *him* exposed. If there's a recipe or script for these things he fit the role as if he'd been born to it …or it had been written around him. Everything suddenly took on new meaning. Aloof and unattached translated to *deviant* and *antisocial,* self-defense just a euphemism for *violent tendencies* …"promiscuous" and "immoral," …he was *the other man*, and the kind who wouldn't go away when told to …obsessed and dangerous, **aka** stalker.

You can marginally hide your activities in this day and age, but you can't erase or disown them, and there was DNA of **every** sort on the surface and beneath it that belonged to him. Jake knew it would only be a matter of time before someone came along inquiring about the *married girl*... Once that happened, it was <u>*highly*</u> conceivable no one would be investing too much time or energy in looking beyond him ...*aside* from himself and his two closest friends. And as time would reveal, the people who thought they knew him best, didn't *know* him as well as they *thought*....

The Author Wishes To Thank...

PUBLISHER

Wolf *Xpress*

A subsidiary of North Carolina State University
Bookstores
&
Teri Hellmann, Manager: For her patience, time,
efforts, and tolerance of me...

COVER

The cover image is a photographic representation of
a tattoo collaboration of Nate Allen and more
importantly...

Tattoo Artist *Christy Alexander*
batratcattat@yahoo.com

Photograph by **Jamen Allen**

Graphics and Design
By **John Starbuck,** Marketing & Communications
NC State Bookstores, Campus Enterprises

For additional information visit our online partners @
www.TheCrookedDog.com